SPY DOG
ROCKET RIDER

ANDREW COPE

Illustrated by James de la Rue

PUFFIN

PUFFIN BOOKS

Published by the Penguin Group
Penguin Books Ltd, 80 Strand, London WC2R ORL, England
Penguin Group (USA) Inc., 375 Hudson Street, New York, New York 10014, USA
Penguin Group (Canada), 90 Eglinton Avenue East, Suite 700, Toronto, Ontario, Canada M4P 2Y3
(a division of Pearson Penguin Canada Inc.)
Penguin Ireland, 25 St Stephen's Green, Dublin 2, Ireland (a division of Penguin Books Ltd)
Penguin Group (Australia), 707 Collins Street, Melbourne, Victoria 3008, Australia
(a division of Pearson Australia Group Pty Ltd)
Penguin Books India Pvt Ltd, 11 Community Centre, Panchsheel Park, New Delhi – 110 017, India
Penguin Group (NZ), 67 Apollo Drive, Rosedale, Auckland 0632, New Zealand
(a division of Pearson New Zealand Ltd)
Penguin Books (South Africa) (Pty) Ltd, Block D, Rosebank Office Park, 181 Jan Smuts Avenue,
Parktown North, Gauteng 2193, South Africa

Penguin Books Ltd, Registered Offices: 80 Strand, London WC2R ORL, England

puffinbooks.com

First published 2009
This edition published 2012

001

Set in Bembo
Typeset by Palimpsest Book Production Limited, Falkirk, Stirlingshire
Printed and bound in Great Britain by Clays Ltd, Elcograf S.p.A.

British Library Cataloguing in Publication Data
A CIP catalogue record for this book is available from the British Library

ISBN: 978-0-141-34539-0

www.greenpenguin.co.uk

MIX
Paper from
responsible sources
FSC® C018179
www.fsc.org

Penguin Books is committed to a sustainable
future for our business, our readers and our planet.
This book is made from Forest Stewardship
Council™ certified paper.

PUFFIN BOOKS

SPY DOG

ROCKET RIDER

Place your finger in the middle of a map of Great Britain. That's exactly where Andrew Cope lives with his wife, children and pet dog Lara. Andrew's family adopted Lara from the RSPCA when she was a tiny pup. They kept feeding her and she grew into something a bit unusual. In fact, Andrew used to call Lara 'ugly' until it was pointed out to him that owners look like their dogs. Andrew has since changed his mind. He now describes Lara as completely gorgeous, super-sophisticated and highly intelligent. There's even a chance that she could be undercover as the world's one and only spy dog.

If you want Lara or her puppy to visit your school, please email her at lara@artofbrilliance.co.uk. They'll probably have to bring Andrew Cope along too, but don't let that put you off. Or you can find out more about the Spy Dog and Spy Pups books online at *www.spydog451.co.uk*, where there are pictures, videos and competitions too!

For my favourite nephews and nieces:
Marconi, The Great Lorenzo, Hayles, Spud,
Jimmy Jango, Mog and Mel

Thanks to:

Tamsin and Bill at Coombeshead Farm, Cornwall – 4,000 words in a day! Best ever. Thanks for the peace and quiet.

Goldfields Academy . . . peaceful and productive African evenings.

Proofreader and ideas consultant, Lou. You were right about the baddie. He was far too nice. Now he's so evil he makes me shiver!

Ollie and Scrump, for test marketing the first draft.

The extraordinary publishing team, especially Shannon, a Kiwi in a Puffin world!

James de la Rue . . . what brilliant illustrations. Thanks for bringing the story to life. I wish I could draw!

All the children who have written or emailed . . . thanks for liking my books! I hope you enjoy reading *Rocket Rider* as much as I've enjoyed writing it.

Contents

0. Space Trivia

Definitely true ...

Neil Armstrong was the first person to set foot on the moon. This was a major step for Neil and a giant leap for humankind. All this happened way before you were born.

Still 100% true ...

A lesser-known fact is that Neil Armstrong was beaten in the space race ... by a dog. The Russians and the Americans were competing to see which nation would be the first to reach the moon. Nobody was quite sure what space was like. Would it be safe for humans? Would aliens shoot down our spaceships? Was the moon really made of cheese?

In the early days of space exploration, it

was too dangerous to send humans, so the Russians sent a dog. Three dogs made the shortlist – Albina, Mushka and Laika. A top Russian scientist was in charge of deciding which dog would be the first animal ever to venture into space.

More facts ...

The Russians selected Laika. She was a supremely intelligent stray dog with silly-looking ears. Laika was three years old when they strapped her into her seat in the Russian

Laika the space dog

rocket *Sputnik 2* and she took off into space. It was a serious leap for doggie-kind!

And one more fact . . .

Laika's body went through enormous pressure as the rocket blasted off. Her pulse rate nearly trebled but she reached orbit and the stray from Moscow became the first ever living creature in space. She ate her dinner as she circled 2,000 miles above the Earth! Imagine the view. That's one awesome mutt!

So what happened to Laika the 'Space Dog'?

It was more than twenty years before Russia decided to tell the world what happened to the first animal that orbited the Earth. The official story is that poor Laika died in space. But after so long how do we know that's the truth? What if she didn't?

What if she's still up there?

What if aliens got her?

And here's an even bigger 'what if?' . . . We know Laika, the Russian stray with funny ears, had enough food to last several days. What if she circled the Earth a few times before following her training and landing her spacecraft in the Atlantic Ocean? What if she was picked up by a Russian ship? Everything was top secret so the scientist and Laika could have slipped out of the country and retired somewhere else in the world. What if the scientist continued to work with Laika, attempting to produce dogs with supreme intelligence? Laika's descendants could still be alive today!

As for the truth? Sometimes it is stranger than fiction.

1. Family Tree

The animal neighbourhood watch team was shaping up well. Lara had recruited fourteen dogs, five cats, two guinea pigs and a tortoise. There hadn't been a single reported crime in the last six months.

Scottie could now bounce on the trampoline and get through upstairs windows, so Lara had put him in charge of search and rescue. Rex had been transformed from a wagging machine to a fighting machine. As the biggest dog, he'd been taught to growl and bare his teeth at the first sign of trouble.

'I know you're a big softie on the inside,' woofed Lara, 'but sometimes you can fool people into thinking you're hard by looking tough on the outside.'

Patch had the loudest bark, so he was in

charge of emergency signalling. Three Patch barks was the signal for danger. A Patch howl was the call for a meeting. A Patch 'howl, bark, bark, howl' meant he needed a wee! Cindy was the fastest, so she was allocated the role of chief fetcher and carrier. If there were any long-distance messages to get to the other side of town, Cindy was proud to take them.

The animals had been transformed from a ramshackle bunch of pets to a highly trained neighbourhood watch unit. And Lara, their leader, watched proudly over them.

Their commander-in-chief was officially retired from active service as a spy dog, but old habits die hard. She'd shared a few daring stories with the neighbourhood pets and they were desperate to learn some of the techniques she'd used at spy school.

'The Secret Service still call me by my code name, GM451,' she'd told her wide-eyed audience. In their eyes, Lara was a super-sophisticated highly trained multi-talented hero. A pet that could understand several languages (English, Italian, Russian, Cat and even basic Dolphin!), send emails and drive a car. They'd marvelled when Lara had organized the annual animal neighbourhood watch summer party and she'd been in charge of the barbecue. A while back they'd seen her driving a car through the village and they knew she'd caught several baddies, including an evil dog smuggler and a dastardly diamond robber. To top it all off, their leader had been summoned to Buckingham Palace to receive an honour from the Queen. And now, here she was, Dame Lara, passing on some of her skills to the pet security team.

'OK,' barked Lara, 'inspection parade before we learn a new skill.'

'Cor, a new skill,' woofed Tigger, bouncing with excitement. 'I wonder what she'll teach us today?'

The pets lined up and Lara barked a command of 'Sit!'. Twenty-two animal bottoms hit the grass. The commander watched while George the tortoise took his time, balancing carefully on the bottom of his shell.

One false move and he'll be over on to his back, legs kicking helplessly in the air again, thought Lara.

Lara wandered along the line, nodding in appreciation. 'Nice, Felix,' she said, noting the tabby cat sitting with tummy in and chest out. She raised an eyebrow at Spot, who breathed in and filled his lungs to capacity. 'Excellent,' she nodded. 'And chin up, old fella.'

Lara reached the end of the line and nodded again approvingly. 'At ease,' she commanded as a few tummies sagged in relief. 'Today's lesson,' she woofed, 'is bike riding.'

George was so shocked that he toppled backwards and his scaly legs started to pump in slow motion. Patch nosed the reptile back up and George's head disappeared indoors in shame.

'George, you're excused,' Lara woofed reassuringly. 'I have something extra special lined up for you.' A grey head appeared from the shell and a tail at the other end. Lara could almost see it wagging in excitement.

'You never know when you'll need extra speed and this represents a possible solution,' said Lara, pointing to one of the bikes she'd brought to the meeting. 'And for those with shorter legs you might like to try this model,' she suggested, jabbing her paw towards a three-wheeled one. 'Now . . . who's up first?' she barked. 'How about you, Jake? You're the same size as me so I can hold you while you get going.'

Jake's eye twitched, part in excitement and part in fear. Lara had nominated him because the slightly mad Labrador was always full of beans. *I need a risk taker*, she thought.

'No problem, boss,' he yapped excitedly. 'The least I can do is give it my best shot.'

'That's the spirit,' encouraged Lara, fixing a cycling helmet to Jake's bony head. Lara wheeled the bike to the far end of the garden. 'Pedals to go. Brake to stop. And handlebars for steering,' she woofed. 'The bike is designed for humans so the brakes can be tricky, but I'm certain you'll get the hang of it.'

Jake nodded. He'd been chosen and was so proud.

Lara held the bike while the Labrador climbed aboard. He rested his feet on the pedals and his front paws on the handlebars.

'Ready?' barked Lara.

'As I'll ever be,' replied Jake, his back legs shaking a little.

'And away we go,' woofed Lara, standing on her hind legs and giving the saddle a little shove forward. The pet audience applauded as Jake's legs began to pump and he wobbled his way out of the garden gate. The animals rushed out into the cul-de-sac to watch, George taking up the rear. They marvelled as Lara trotted behind Jake for a little while and then held their breath as she let go. The bike wobbled but Jake stayed aboard as he gathered pace down the hill.

'I'm doing it, Lara!' he yapped. 'But don't let go, will you?'

Lara looked at the assembled crowd and shrugged. *Too late for that*, she thought.

'How do I stop again?' came a rather worried woof.

'The brakes,' barked Lara from afar. 'Pull the lever and you'll stop.'

At this point the assembled team learnt a valuable lesson. 'Never look backwards when you're riding a bike,' Lara explained as Jake's nose pointed towards them. 'Otherwise you'll lose your balance.'

All eyes went back to Jake. His legs had now left the pedals and the wobbles seemed uncontrollable. He weaved between two lamp posts and narrowly missed a wheelie bin before hitting number 27's hedge at some speed. They heard a howl and watched Jake's back legs disappear over the hedge and then a splash as he landed in the paddling pool.

'And lesson number two,' barked Lara, 'don't apply the front brakes too hard.'

A soggy Jake emerged from number 27.

A huge round of applause greeted him as he trotted back to the team. George had made it to the gate but missed all the action. 'What happened?' he asked, his tortoise eyes shining.

'Jake here has just become the world's *second* bike-riding dog,' Lara told him. 'He needs a bit more practice, especially at stopping, but boy has he got potential.'

Jake shook himself dry and sat proudly.

George was pleased for Jake but he couldn't help feeling a bit jealous. He'd spoken to Lara about his need for speed and she'd devised a special training programme and diet to enhance his athletic ability. By tortoise standards George was a real mover but he had no chance of keeping up with the rest of the team.

'And one last thing,' woofed Lara. 'I said I had something extra special for George.' All eyes turned to the tortoise and he sat tall on the end of his shell. Lara opened a wooden box and produced a skateboard and harness. 'George now has some wheels. With a bit of practice, he is about to become the fastest tortoise in the world!'

George toppled over again, his chunky legs waving about in the air.

Bless him, thought Lara. *The excitement's just too much.*

The meeting broke up and the animals left, many chatting excitedly. Lara smiled with pride. *Sure, they're a bit rough round the edges. But what courage. And teamwork. And enthusiasm!*

Her two-year intensive spy-dog training had secured her place as top dog ... by a mile. But the best of the rest was Potter. He was her favourite. As the rest of the animals disappeared, Potter sat wagging enthusiastically. A handsome black shaggy pedigree with shining eyes, Potter was a good all-rounder with a positive attitude and Lara was grooming him to be second-in-command.

'That was another great meeting,' barked Potter. 'I love the fact you've designed some wheels for George. When he gets the hang of them he'll be the fastest tortoise ever!'

'That's just phase one,' woofed Lara. 'I've asked Professor Cortex to design an extra-special gadget,' she explained. 'He'll be transformed into a supertortoise.'

'Wow!' said Potter. 'He'll be so excited.'

Lara smiled a doggie smile as she and Potter trotted side by side. Her thoughts turned to another subject – something that she'd been spending a lot of time thinking about in the last few days.

'Potter,' she asked, 'can I ask you about family?'

Potter listened hard, the sound of doggie paws tapping on the pavement.

'Do you know who your mum and dad are?' woofed Lara.

'Well, I don't get to see them,' replied Potter, 'but I have certificates to say who they are and I know where they live.'

'And aren't you curious about seeing them?' Lara woofed.

The dogs stopped at the crossing and Lara pressed the button.

'Not really,' admitted Potter. 'I have a brilliant family. My owners are the best ever and I love them to bits.'

The green man beeped and Lara looked right and left before crossing the road. 'I love mine too,' she agreed. 'Being a family pet is wonderful. It's just that I don't have certificates. I don't know who my parents are or where they're from. Or even if they're still alive.' The dogs walked together towards their homes. It was a chilly evening and the drizzle made it look a bit misty. 'I'm the happiest dog in the world. It just makes me wonder, that's all,' thought Lara aloud.

'I don't think you should wonder too much, Lara,' wagged Potter. 'Dogs aren't supposed to wonder. Have you heard the phrase "man's best friend"? That's what we should focus on. Find a great family and then be man's best friend.'

'And women and children,' added Lara. 'I know you're right, Potter. But I don't even have a name. The Secret Service gave me a reference number. I'm just "GM451". OK, so it says "LARA" on my collar but that just stands for "Licensed Assault and

Rescue Animal". I sometimes wonder what my parents named me ... and who they are.'

The dogs trotted in silence for a couple of minutes. Lara's mind was racing with thoughts of her family. She'd lived with Mr and Mrs Cook and their children – Ben, Sophie and Ollie – since they'd adopted her from the RSPCA almost a year ago.

Well, technically it was me that chose them, she thought, *but I always let them think it was the other way around. And I can't believe how well I've settled in and how lucky I am to have the best family a dog could wish for.* Lara cast her mind back to her spy-dog days. *Of course, working for the Secret Service was exciting,* she thought. *But being a family pet is so much more rewarding. And we've had plenty of adventures too. It's not that I go looking for adventure ... it sort of seeks me out!*

Lara and Potter arrived at the Cooks' house. It was late and the lights were out. Lara pressed the numbers on the security pad and opened the door. Potter shook his shaggy coat and wiped his feet before padding into the house.

'Can you stay a while?' asked Lara. 'And talk about your family?'

'I'd love to,' woofed Potter. The two dogs snuggled in Lara's basket and chatted long into the night.

2. Gadget Heaven

Professor Cortex was thoroughly enjoying his break from spy school. 'Real school is brilliant,' he told Lara. 'I adore teaching. And, I'll tell you this, GM451, the children are such willing volunteers.'

The professor was a workaholic. The school bell went at 3.15 p.m. but his science classroom was lit up most of the night as he huddled over experiments. The professor wasn't really a teacher at all. He'd spent the last forty years working for the Secret Service, heading up the animal spy school where Lara had trained. Lara always thought that he put the 'mad' in 'mad professor'.

Not everyone understood his lessons but there was no doubting they were fun. His science classes involved a series of explosions, potions and inventions. His love of the subject came across in everything he did. When he covered a maths session he taught the children about Einstein. In geography he built a volcano that spewed out popcorn and in music the children had learnt the theme tune to *Doctor Who*.

Ben, Sophie, Ollie and Lara were ushered into the science lab on a Sunday morning. Professor Cortex was very excited, rubbing his hands in anticipation and hopping about in what Sophie called the 'mad professor dance'.

'I'm sooo delighted you could make it so early,' beamed the professor, ignoring the fact that Ben was wiping sleep from his eyes. 'I don't have a spy school any more, but that hasn't stopped me experimenting. And I've got some wonderful inventions to show you.'

The children perked up a bit. They loved the James Bond-style gadgets that the professor came up with. Ben had some night-vision goggles and Ollie had a football with a built-in listening device. He'd used it to discover the name of Ben's new girlfriend!

'Look at this, children.' Their science

teacher ushered the group over to a large metal box and circled his hands as if doing a magic spell. 'This is an animal cleaner. It's going to be called a "Pet-o-Matic",' he announced proudly, emphasizing the 'o'. 'It will make us millions of pounds that I can then reinvest in further experiments. Total simplicity. Imagine a car wash, but for pets.'

Lara took a step back. *A dog washer? No way, Prof.*

The professor noticed Lara backing away. 'Don't be so negative, GM451. Come on, have a go. It's very quick, almost painless and very safe.'

Almost painless? thought Lara, cocking her head in alarm. *Did you say 'almost'?*

The professor had already opened the back of the machine and switched it on. He took Lara in his arms and heaved her on to the conveyor belt at one end of the machine. 'Takes less than a minute,' he assured them as Lara disappeared into the metal box. 'Ears and tail down, if possible!' he shouted after her. 'You always have to put your aerial down in a car wash,' he reminded the children. 'Same principle here.'

'What's happening in there?' asked Ollie as they heard a few muffled yelps.

'Cleaning every nook and cranny,' enthused the professor. 'And now she's being rinsed and blow-dried,' he explained as the fans began to hum.

The children moved to the other end of the machine, waiting for their beloved pet to come safely off the conveyor belt. Their eyes were drawn to the red blinking light.

'This is in its early stages of development,' explained the professor while they waited. 'But in the next few years, every pet owner will have one. No more muddy paw prints or wet carpets. And it's not just for dogs, oh no, siree. Cats, hamsters, guinea pigs,' he counted. 'Maybe parrots? Possibly big "Pet-o-Matic"'s in zoos too,' he thought aloud. 'Lions, elephants, zebras ... that kind of thing. It's totally revolutionary.'

The red light was replaced by green and the conveyor rumbled into action. Lara's fluffy head was the first part to emerge. She had a wild look on her face and both ears were down. Her body emerged, fluffed up ridiculously by the dryer.

Ben gasped at his pet. 'She's twice the size!' he shouted. 'And she smells of . . . peaches and apples,' he said, sniffing loudly.

Lara's white fur shone and her black patches were like the night. Her teeth sparkled and her nails glinted. Her ear flicked back up, daylight showing through the bullet hole. The family pet let out a low whistle. *Wow! Nice one, Prof*, she nodded, catching her reflection in the mirror. *I'm glowing on the inside and outside. I like the fluffy look. And what great fun.*

'Can you do one for humans?' asked Ollie excitedly. 'I could go in it before school and it'd only take me a minute and I'd have more time in bed and –'

'Humans?' exclaimed Professor Cortex. 'You

always come up with the most amazing suggestions,' he said, spitting with enthusiasm. 'Yes, indeed. Why not people?' he thought aloud, scribbling 'People-o-Matic' on a pad.

The children followed the professor to the next table. Ollie was beaming and the mad professor dance had become catching.

'GM451 asked me to come up with something for George, the neighbourhood watch tortoise,' said the professor. 'We came up with a design for wheels. How's he doing with them?'

All eyes fell on the family pet. Her fluffy head nodded encouragingly. *I've seen him practising. Scarily fast*, she agreed, *especially downhill*.

'This little beauty represents phase two for George,' beamed the professor, holding up a small rocket. 'He'll be a hundred-mile-an-hour tortoise! Imagine this skateboard is George,' explained the scientist, fixing the rocket to the top of the board. 'And get a load of this!' The children followed as Professor Cortex marched out into the corridor, bent down and placed the skateboard on to the floor. 'Here goes ... three, two, one ... blast-off!'

The rocket ignited and the skateboard leapt forward, nought to a hundred in less than a second. The skateboard rocketed through the corridor and hit the wall with such force that it shattered into a hundred pieces. Everyone ducked for cover as the rocket exploded and the corridor filled with smoke. Lara bounded over to the crash scene and aimed a fire extinguisher at the flames.

Poor old George, she thought. *I think a bit more tweaking is required before he moves to phase two!*

The professor looked a little disappointed. 'Perhaps a few more adjustments,' he nodded. 'But let's focus on the positives. George does have a shell.'

Professor Cortex marched back to his lab, undeterred by the failure of George's rocket. 'I think you'll find this interesting, GM451,' he beamed, throwing the dog a piece of material. 'It's a special arctic suit that will protect you in sub-zero temperatures. Tight-fitting Lycra, blue and red, so you'll look a bit like Superman. Except you're a dog, of course. So "Superdog" then,' he chuckled. 'Do you want to try it on?'

Lara raised a you-must-be-mad-thinking-I'm-going-to-wear-this-ridiculous-looking-outfit eyebrow. *No way, Prof,* she thought. *I'm not a superhero. I'm a family pet, remember? What will my chums think if I turn up at the park in a sparkly outfit with pants on the outside? One hundred per cent no chance.*

Sophie giggled, imagining her pet in the outfit.

Don't even think it, glared the dog.

'OK, GM451, I'm picking up the vibes that you perhaps won't wear the Lycra suit. Too cool for your own good sometimes,' he nagged. 'Tell you what, everyone, let's have a break. Who fancies a drink?' The children's hands shot up and the professor led the way to the drinks machine in the dinner hall.

I'll be along in a minute, woofed Lara. *I've just got to smooth my fur a bit. I don't want Potter to see me like this!* Lara stood on her hind legs and peered in the mirror. She licked her paws before patting down her fluffy fringe. There was a bottle of water on the desk so she wandered over to take a sip. *This automatic dog-cleaning technology has made me thirsty!* Lara unscrewed the top with her teeth, grabbed the bottle with her mouth and took some gulps of water.

The professor's files were scattered over the table and she noticed one marked 'GM451 – CONFIDENTIAL'. Lara grimaced and shook her head. *It's private*, she thought. *So I shouldn't.* She sipped some more water before her eyes came back to the file. *But it's about me, so maybe I should?* She padded over to the door and peered out. *Nobody around. What harm can it do? The professor wouldn't have left the file out on the table if it was so secret.*

Lara jumped up to the table and opened the file. She licked her paw and flicked through a few pages. Her eyes widened as she looked at some of the headings: 'Training', 'Spy School Scores', 'Gadgets', she read. Lara flicked over another page and her eyes widened. 'Family History!' The dog let out a low whistle. *Wow!* she thought. *This is dynamite!*

3. Secret Files

Lara's heart was pounding. She knew she shouldn't be reading a top-secret file but the temptation was too much. She trotted to the door and stood with her head cocked. *The coast's clear.* Lara padded back to the table, licked her paw again and turned the pages of the secret file.

There was a lot of information, including graphs and performance league tables. She smiled as she saw just how far ahead she was of the other dogs at spy training school. *It really was no contest!*

Lara flicked through a few more pages of data. She checked her IQ score. *Mmm, better than most humans*, she reflected. She checked out her fitness graphs. *Whoops*, she thought, following the downward line. *I really must*

cut down on custard creams! But it was the last page that caught her attention. The professor's handwriting was spidery and faint but there was no mistaking the words 'Family history'. Lara's heart quickened. She thought about Potter and his family tree. *Maybe this is what I'm after,* she thought. *Maybe I can find out who my parents are. I might even be able to meet them.* Lara ran her paw over the spidery writing . . .

The puppy was discovered in a small
flat in London. Her elderly owner was
ill and was taken to a care home. The
puppy was incredibly bright. Unnaturally
so. News got to me and I acquired the

28

dog for spy school. Code name GM451.
Commonly Known as LARA: 'Licensed
Assault and Rescue Animal'.

Lara read on. She knew the next bit.

GM451 responded well to the training.
A super dog indeed. But clearly super
before she reached me. Excelled in all
tests. Can't speak but can understand
English and several other languages. Can
send emails and surf the net. Can drive
a car, ride a bike, etc. Decent footballer.
Graduated as the world's first 'spy dog'
and was employed on special missions by
the Secret Service. One of GM451's
missions went wrong and she followed the
orders I gave her. She got deliberately
captured by the RSPCA and adopted a
family. She chose Mr and Mrs Cook and
their three children. Nice family. Great
Kids.

Lara smiled. *They sure are.* She took another
swig of water without taking her eyes off
the diary.

Some mishap while with the Cooks. Dreadful business but she had no choice but to protect the family. GM451 drawn into an adventure that resulted in her being shot. Five bullets. One through her upright ear, giving her a distinctive look. One bullet still lodged in her. Deemed too unfit to return to active spy service so allowed to stay with her adopted family.

Current status - semi-retired

Current objective - to keep GM451 up to date with gadgets and training should she ever need to carry out more missions.

Lara's ears pricked as she heard footsteps coming down the corridor.

Ollie shouted, 'We've got a milkshake for you, Lara. A banana one. Are you coming to drink it with us?'

The family pet quickly turned the page and read the last paragraph.

GM451's canine family? Information unknown. Previous owner, Oleg Jetski, was traced to the Elms Care Home. Ex-Russian scientist and astronaut. Interesting background but he's very ill. Interviewed but shows no movement or speech. He holds the key to GM451's history, but it seems the secret is lost. Case closed.

Case closed! thought Lara, reading the final passage several more times. *Case closed! This old man knows who my parents were. He may even know where they are right now. He holds the secret. Consider the case reopened!*

Ollie burst into the science lab and Lara snapped the folder shut. *Banana milkshake*, she nodded. *My fave*, wagged the family pet, licking her lips. Lara trotted along the corridor to join her adopted family. She loved them more than anything else in the whole world. *But I have to know the truth. I need to find Mr Jetski.*

4. Action Plan

It was Monday evening and the boys were glued to the TV. Mum stomped in, hands on hips, and tutted at the advert.

'Jimmy's Tartan Suncream,' began the beaming Jimmy. 'Special formula, special strength ... ointment for those oh-so-important ozone moments ...' he continued, teeth glinting at the camera.

'"Ozone moments" indeed,' mimicked Mum. 'It's February, for heaven's sake. Why are we having suncream ads in winter? Anyway, you three,' she barked, 'it's homework moments I'm interested in.' The boys moaned loudly as Mum clicked the Off button and pocketed the remote. 'No more telly until all homework is finished.'

Sophie never needed ordering, she was

happy to knuckle down. The boys would perch, transfixed, in front of the Wii while Sophie sat like a snake charmer, practising her clarinet.

Ollie's homework was always really easy, but then he had only just turned six so Lara wasn't sure he should even be getting homework at all. Because he had a short attention span Lara had to play homework games to make it seem more interesting. As a result, he'd giggled his way through storywriting and Lara had made him sit in the game show 'hot seat' while he practised his two times table.

Ben hummed the suncream jingle as he made his way to Dad's office to Google his homework. Lara joined him.

Science, she noticed. *Excellent. That's my favourite subject.* Lara watched patiently as Ben searched for information on global warming. Lara knew she was officially the family pet, but it was the eleven-year-old who loved her the most. They played endless hours of football. Recently Ben had taken up rugby at his new school so Lara had swapped her goalie gloves for a mouthguard and shoulder pads. She had become expert at rugby tackling.

'Aim for the knees!' Ben always shouted. 'Doesn't matter how big you are, you can't run without knees.' The two would often come in from the garden, muddied and hungry, then chomp prawn cocktail crisps in front of a DVD.

Lara took the seat next to him and watched him research his homework.

'Hi, girl,' said Ben as he reached to stroke his pet. 'What can I do for you?'

I need a huge favour, thought the dog. Lara took a pencil in her mouth, opened Word and began to tap out a message on the computer. Ben looked confused. 'A Russian

astronaut?' he said. 'In a care home? And you want to do *what*?'

It was at times like this that Lara really wished she could speak. *Pencil-typing is so slow and frustrating.* She reread the message. *That's about it*, she thought, putting on her sad eyes and pleading with little whimpers. *Please, Ben, I need your help.*

Ben called a meeting in his bedroom. Ollie took no persuading as his big brother's tone of voice made it sound much more exciting than homework. Sophie sat on the edge of the bed, her arms round Lara.

Ben closed the door but remained standing. This was a leadership moment. 'OK,' he began, keeping his voice down. 'Lara's got a big secret and she needs our help.' Ollie stopped lounging and sat up straight. 'As you know, we adopted Lara from the RSPCA when she was a pup. And we know she's a spy dog.'

'Retired,' corrected Sophie.

'Retired spy dog,' agreed Ben. 'Well, it seems there's a chance that Lara can find her original owner. The person who might know about her past. Her mum and dad, even!'

Sophie gasped in horror and gripped her pet tighter.

'Don't worry,' said Ben quickly, 'that doesn't mean she's going to leave us. But it will help her piece together her past. Isn't that right, girl?'

The family pet nodded solemnly. *I'm never ever going to leave you*, she thought. *But I hope you understand that I need to satisfy my curiosity. And, Sophie, can you please stop squeezing me so hard?*

'So, where's her owner?' asked Ollie.

'He's a very old man, in a care home,' explained Ben. 'About twenty miles from here.'

'And how are we going to go twenty miles?' snorted Ollie.

'Here's the plan,' said Ben, passing his brother and sister a piece of paper. 'Lara's worked it all out. This Saturday. A bike ride and two buses.'

'Cool,' exclaimed Ollie. 'This is like a real adventure!'

'But how exactly do we get Lara into the

care home?' asked the ever-practical Sophie.

'Don't worry,' said Ben. 'Every detail's been taken care of. Remember, this is top secret. All Mum needs to know is that we're going for a bike ride and we'll need a picnic.'

Ollie's eyes glowed with excitement. 'Is this a real mission?'

'It's a *top-secret* mission,' reminded Ben. 'So keep it zipped.'

5. The Silent Legend

Ollie scoffed his breakfast even faster than normal. Lara picked at her Saturday morning bacon and eggs, too nervous to eat. 'Remind me where exactly it is you're riding to?' asked Mum, her hands plunged into soapy suds as she washed up.

All eyes fell on Ben – he'd been assigned to do the talking. 'Through the village and along the cycle path to the river,' he said, trying to sound matter-of-fact. 'So there's no traffic,' he added, knowing this would convince his mum.

'Be careful at the river, won't you?' she reminded, drying her hands. 'And you're in charge,' she nodded at Lara with a smile. 'No mischief. No danger. And absolutely no adventures!'

I'll be on my best behaviour, Mrs C, wagged the family pet. *It's just a fact-finding mission. No chance of danger, honest!*

The cycle ride was easy. Lara wasn't allowed to ride a bike in case strangers saw her.

'A bike-riding mutt is just going to draw attention,' agreed Ben.

So she lolloped alongside the children, enjoying the keep-fit opportunity. They dismounted at the railway bridge and Ben chained the bikes up. He disappeared for a couple of minutes and came back wheeling a suitcase. Lara wagged her tail excitedly. 'It's exactly where I hid it yesterday,' he beamed.

Ben wheeled the suitcase to the bus stop and they all caught two buses in the direction of the Elms Care Home.

Once they got off at the right stop, Ben unzipped the suitcase. 'Now for the tricky bit. Lara, in you get.'

Lara climbed into the empty case and scrunched herself inside. *It's a bit cramped,* she thought, *but it's the only way I'm going to get inside the care home.*

Ben zipped up the case and left a bit open so air could get in.

'OK in there?' asked Ollie.

A bit uncomfortable, came a muffled bark. *But let's get going.*

Ben, Sophie and Ollie approached the door of the Elms Care Home, trundling the suitcase behind them. Lara felt herself being bumped along the pavement and then her cheeks wobbled as the case was hauled across some cobbles before finally coming to rest.

She pricked up her ears and listened. *We must be here. Be confident, Ben!*

Ollie pointed to the *No dogs* sign and gave his brother a worried look.

'Don't worry, Ollie. Lara won't make a noise.' Ben smoothed his hair and clothes before knocking on the huge black door. The children waited nervously for someone to open it.

They were just about to give up when the door was answered by a lady with a vacuum cleaner in her hand. She wiped her forearm across her face, scraping the strands of hair away. 'Yes, children?' she enquired, switching off her machine. 'What can I do for you?'

Ben felt awkward. 'Erm, do you have a Mr Jetski staying here?' he asked. 'It's just that I'm doing a project about space and I wanted to chat to him.'

The lady eyed the children suspiciously. 'Space, m'dear?' she asked. 'What do you mean "space"?'

'We think he's an expert on space travel. You know, man on the moon stuff,' chirped Ben.

The lady thought for a moment. Mr Jetski's

41

room was plastered with pictures of spacecraft and planets. 'Are you a relative?' she asked.

'No, just an admirer. He's had an exciting life and our friend Lara knows him and we need to see him. That's all,' blurted Ben.

The lady didn't look convinced. 'And where's your "friend" Lara?' she asked.

'Er, I'm Lara,' said Sophie, stepping forward to hold out her hand. She hated lying but she knew how important this was to their pet.

Lara gasped silently from inside the suitcase and she heard Ollie squeak as he received a nudge in the ribs from his sister.

The lady shook 'Lara's' hand. She was busy and didn't have time to stand around talking. 'Come on in, then,' she said. 'Mr Jetski needs as many admirers as he can get. I'm afraid he's in a bit of a bad way. I can let you into his room but can't let you stay long. He had a massive stroke six months ago and hardly ever speaks. To be honest, it's sad to see the man in such a state. Maybe your visit will do him some good.'

Lara crossed her paws for luck as the suitcase followed the lady along the corridor. She could hear the children's trainers squeaking on the shiny floor and the smell of hospitals reminded her of her time as a spy dog when she had been seriously ill.

They went past a big lounge and Ollie peered in at the elderly people sitting watching TV. The advert for Jimmy's Tartan Suncream was blaring out with its annoying jingle. One old lady was sitting in her chair lifting her legs up and down, doing a sort of armchair aerobics, but the others looked as though they were snoozing.

'He's not in there,' said the lady, marching onwards. 'He's too ill to leave his room. By the way,' asked the lady, 'what's in the case?'

'Erm, holiday stuff,' said Sophie quickly, trying to sound carefree. 'We're going on holiday after we've met Mr Jetski.'

'Oh,' said the lady. 'Where are you going?'

'Devon,' 'Blackpool,' 'Australia,' the children said at the same time.

'We're doing a kind of tour,' smiled Ben nervously. 'Starting in Devon and ending in Australia.'

The lady stopped at a door at the end of

the corridor, hand on the handle. 'Gosh, that's quite a holiday. Now,' she soothed, 'I don't want you to be shocked at what you see. Please bear in mind that Mr Jetski is a very old man indeed. Not only is he old but also very ill. He's lost most of his speech and movement. But he can understand you all right. It's just that you might have to do all the talking.' She took a deep breath, put on a positive face and breezed through the door. 'Good morning, Mr J,' she chirped. 'I've brought you some visitors – some children. They say they're big fans of yours. This young man is doing a project about space travel or something. Is that OK? I'll leave you with Lara and, er …'

'Ben,' said Ben, 'Oh, and this is Ollie.'

'I'll leave you and Lara and Ben and Ollie together for five minutes so they can talk to you …' she glanced at Ben, 'for a school magazine or something.'

Ben nodded and the lady left the room as swiftly as she entered, closing the door behind her. The room was almost empty, except for a bed, table, wheelchair and a small armchair by the window. But the walls were covered in photos of rockets and planets. Ollie's eyes lit up with excitement.

Mr Jetski was sitting near the window looking out over the garden.

Ben was beginning to wonder what on earth he was going to say. And Mr Jetski couldn't say much, so it was going to be a very one-sided conversation. He approached the old man hesitantly. 'Hello, Mr Jetski,' he began. 'Or is it OK to call you "Oleg"?'

There was no response. Mr Jetski continued to gaze out of the window, watching the birds peck at a bag of nuts hanging from the bird table. He was a rather shrunken man with a bushy grey moustache, furry eyebrows and a bald head.

'I don't think he can hear you,' hissed Sophie.

Ben looked round at his sister, frowning for her to shush. 'But the thing I really wanted to tell you was that we've brought someone special to see you. A dog.' Ben thought he saw a flicker of emotion from the old man's face and decided to carry on.

'I see you like dogs, Mr Jetski,' he said,

his eyes drawn to a photo of a black and white dog in a picture frame. 'We've had to smuggle her into your room because dogs aren't allowed. She's hidden,' he continued, nodding at the suitcase. 'And she's a spy!'

And uncomfortable, whined a small noise from inside the bag. *Can someone please let me out!*

Ben waited for a response. His voice dropped in disappointment. 'I just thought you ought to know, that's all.'

'Mr Waterski, you had her when she was a puppy,' smiled Ollie. 'When she was dead cute.'

What do you mean 'was'? huffed Lara.

'Laika's great-granddaughter?' mumbled Mr Jetski, lifting an ancient hand and pointing to the framed picture.

Sophie wheeled the suitcase over to the window and got to work on the zip.

Lara uncoiled her body and stretched, thankful to be out of the confined space. *Who's Laika?* she thought.

Ben picked up the black and white picture and turned it towards Lara. 'Your great-grandma,' he grinned. 'Look, silly ears and everything.'

Lara was about to get annoyed when there was a knock at the door and in breezed a nurse, looking faintly surprised that the children were there.

Lara dived behind a curtain and held her breath. *If I'm discovered we'll be thrown out for sure.*

The nurse was carrying what looked like a child's juice bottle, shaking it vigorously. 'Good morning, Mr Jetski,' she shouted, as though he was deaf. 'I see you have visitors. I've brought you your tea, dear,' she continued, showing him the baby bottle. No response. 'I'll just leave it here for a minute to cool down and then come back and feed you, all right?' said the nurse, as if speaking to a child. 'Or do you want one of your grandchildren to feed you? And it's terribly gloomy in here. Do you want me to let some sunshine in for you?' She took hold of the curtains, threatening to reveal the family pet.

Lara's paw was over her face. *No, no, please don't spoil everything!* she cringed.

'It's OK,' blurted Sophie. 'We'll do that for him when we leave.'

The lady nodded and let go of the curtain. The children were filled with relief as she left the room.

'Phew, that was close,' gasped Sophie.

It's not over yet, thought Lara as she emerged from behind the curtain. *I may have been hidden from her, but not him!* The gardener had spied her in Mr Jetski's room and the children watched as he marched up to the window and banged loudly.

'What's that dog doing in there?' came the muffled voice. 'This is a dog-free zone. Please open the window so I can talk to you.'

Lara knew it was rude but she couldn't help

sticking her paws in her ears and waggling them at the man. *You're out there and I'm in here,* she crowed. The gardener's face fell into a look of silent shock as Lara stuck out her long doggie tongue and pulled her silliest face before swishing the curtains shut.

'Fine, I'll come inside and get you out, mutt!' came the gardener's muffled voice from behind the closed curtains.

'Oh no,' said Ben.

Lara calculated that they had about ninety seconds to get any information they could from Mr Jetski. *This is so tough!* She stood in front of her former owner and looked him over. She had only been a puppy when she'd been taken away from him but a few of her earliest memories suddenly came flooding back. He had been so kind to her and she knew he loved her. *He's always been ill, even in the old days.* Lara remembered helping him around the house, running errands and doing the crossword together. *But he looks so much older than I remember.* Lara jumped up and put her paws on the old man's knees, planting a wet lick on his cheek.

'He's smiling,' shouted Ollie. 'He knows you, Lara!'

But will he be able to help me? thought Lara, listening to the footsteps marching down the hall. *Before we're discovered.*

6. Decision Time

Lara stared at her first owner. *There's certainly a spark in his eye*, she thought. The gardener was shouting as he came down the corridor and she knew time was short. *If we're caught, we're going to be in big trouble.*

'Lara says you looked after her when she was a puppy,' explained Ben. 'She's keen to know her history. She's a spy dog, see. The only one of her kind. She's been taught by Professor Cortex but she was special even before he trained her. Lara really wants to know why. And she wants to know if she's got a family.'

'I mean, she's got us,' added Sophie. 'And we love her to bits. But has she got any doggie family? You know, brothers and sisters or a mum and dad of her own?'

And we've got about fifteen seconds before we have a big problem, urged Lara, listening as the stomping got louder.

Everyone stared at Mr Jetski. Lara's big brown eyes were pleading. *If there's anything you can share with me, please do.*

'The diary in the desk,' mumbled the old man in a thick Russian accent. 'It has whole story. Very special dog.'

Sophie opened a drawer and picked out an old leather book. 'This?'

The old man nodded slowly, the effort almost too much for him. 'Take it,' he croaked. 'You must go now.'

Ben stuffed the diary into his jacket pocket and looked at Lara for inspiration.

Well, we can't go that way, she thought, listening to the footsteps pounding ever closer. Sophie locked the door to buy some time but there was a loud knock and the children looked at each other in alarm. The door handle turned and rattled in frustration.

'Let us in,' bellowed a man's voice. 'We know you're in there. Let us in or we'll break down the door.'

Yikes, thought Lara. *There's only one other*

way out. She helped Ben open the window as wide as it would go. *A bit of a tight squeeze*, frowned Lara as she looked at the gap. She breathed in and wondered if it was *too* tight.

Sophie and Ollie were first through. 'Run!' said Ben. 'Don't wait for us. You next, Lara. I can help you.'

Lara nodded and started to squeeze through the small gap. Her barrel chest got stuck and her back legs kicked wildly as she struggled through the window. She landed with a bit of a thud. *Made it*, she woofed, dusting herself down.

Ben pushed the empty suitcase through

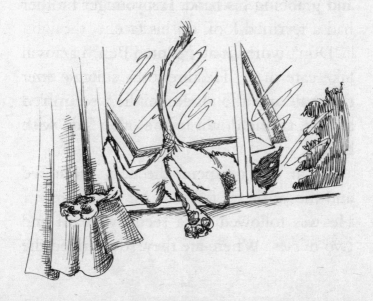

the gap and started to climb through after it. *Come on, lad*, Lara urged. *By the sound of it the gardener is throwing himself at the door. It won't be long before it gives way.*

Ben glanced at Mr Jetski, to see the old man's eyes shining in excitement. 'Go,' he urged. 'You must go quick.'

Ben mouthed a 'thank you' and wriggled out of the window as Mr Jetski pulled a cord and closed the curtains. Ben could see his sister and brother up ahead, sprinting across the lawn. Lara had taken off like a greyhound and climbed the wall. She dangled her paw, ready to help the children up. Ben ran faster than he'd ever run before, soon catching Ollie and grabbing his hand. His younger brother had a terrified look on his face.

'Don't worry, mate,' panted Ben. 'Lara will take care of us.' He threw the suitcase over the wall and the three children scrambled after it, falling down to the other side with Lara.

Just at that moment, the door splintered and the gardener fell into Mr Jetski's room. He was followed by a security guard and two nurses. 'Where are they?' demanded the gardener. 'That pesky dog and those kids?' The security man checked under the bed and behind the curtains.

'Nobody,' he confirmed. 'Just one very old man. And he can't tell us much! Are you sure the mutt was in this room?'

'Course I'm sure,' snapped the gardener. 'It pulled a face at me . . . like this,' he said, sticking his thumbs in his ears and waggling his fingers.

The nurses exchanged worried glances. Maybe the gardener had been in the sunshine too long? One of the nurses closed the window and they all left to check a few other rooms.

Oleg Jetski sat alone, staring at the picture of Laika, a huge grin spread across his face.

Ben led his brother and sister to a cafe with a garden. Lara sat outside while they ordered lemonade and then joined her, Sophie carrying the treasure tightly in her hand. The leather-bound diary was put in front of Lara and all eyes fell on the family pet.

'It's your history, Lara,' said Ben. 'So you should be the first to read it.'

I've waited so long to find out who my parents are, thought Lara. *Here we go . . .*

The children sipped their drinks in silence as Lara opened the book with her paw and read all about her secret history.

Lara and Potter snuggled up that evening after the neighbourhood watch meeting. The dog basket was perfect for two. Lara wasn't sure where to start. In fact, she wasn't even sure if Potter was interested or would understand. Lara always had to tell herself that Potter was an ordinary dog and she shouldn't expect too much.

'I've found out about my family,' she woofed ever so quietly in the dark. There

was silence, except for the humming of the fridge.

'I bet they're really special dogs,' replied Potter eventually. 'Which explains why you're so amazing.'

'My grandmother was certainly very special,' agreed Lara. She told Potter everything that was in Mr Jetski's diary. How she was related to Laika, the first animal in space. 'She was my great-grandmother.' About how Laika was identified as superintelligent, which was why she was chosen for the mission. And how the Russians had kept Laika's story a secret before eventually reporting that she'd died. 'But she didn't die in space,' explained Lara. 'The diary says she landed safely. Splashed down in the ocean. The Russian government were very secretive because they didn't want anyone else to get their hands on this superdog.' Lara knew the diary off by heart. 'And a Russian astronaut, Oleg Jetski, has kept the line of dogs going through a special breeding programme. He was my first owner but he's very old now,' explained Lara. 'Too old to talk very much. But the diary says I have seven brothers and sisters.' Lara fell silent. The fridge did too.

'And?' woofed Potter. 'A mum and dad?'

'The diary says my dad is still alive. He's called Leo and works as a rescue dog in the Scottish highlands, near their highest mountain, Ben Nevis. Strong as an ox, according to the diary.'

'And what are you going to do?' asked Potter. 'You already have a family that you love.'

'What would you do?'

Potter was thoughtful. 'That's not for me to say,' he added wisely. 'It's something you have to decide.'

Potter drifted off to sleep. Lara's ear stood upright and her eyes shone in the dark. There was only one thing a spy dog could do.

Lara met the professor in his school laboratory early on Sunday morning. 'Good morning, GM451,' he said, without looking up from his Bunsen burner. 'What can I do for you?'

No point beating around the bush, thought Lara, dropping the diary out of her mouth on to the table in front of the old man. She went to the filing cabinet and opened it. The professor watched the dog rummage around before selecting the file marked 'GM451: Confidential'. He coughed and looked a little sheepish. 'Ah,' he spluttered, 'you've been doing your homework. I can explain,' he gabbled, not knowing where to start.

My family, Prof. I've been doing some spy-dog investigations. Why didn't you tell me about my family? Lara took a pencil in her mouth. *my dad in scotland,* she scribbled. *I need to meet him.*

'Impossible,' spluttered the professor. 'That's ancient history, GM451. Your future is here with the Cooks, not in Scotland with a total stranger.'

Lara's mouth gripped the pencil again. *need to c him will u help?*

'Out of the question, GM451!' snapped the professor. 'There's nothing to be gained and everything to be lost. And besides, it'll probably end in a wild goose chase.'

OK, thought Lara, *at least I know where I stand. But this wild goose intends to chase.*

The professor fussed around Lara, trying to persuade her to change her mind. He tutted as she filled a backpack with an assortment of gadgets. He could see she was going to Scotland no matter what he said.

Lara turned to leave and the professor shouted for her to stop. 'It's clear your mind's made up,' he shouted. 'But if you're going to meet your father, at least take this.' He held up a piece of material. 'It's the arctic suit. If I can't stop you, the least I can do is protect you. It'll keep out the cold.'

He packed the suit into Lara's backpack before giving her an awkward hug. Lara nodded her appreciation and bounded off. She had a lot of miles to cover.

7. *Stowaway*

The suncream jingle blasted out and Jimmy held his smile for a full thirty seconds. His eyes took on a look of panic as the smile started to hurt. The cameraman gave the thumbs up and Jimmy relaxed, his face sinking into a more comfortable slump. 'Thanks goodness for that,' he shouted. 'All that smiling was killing me. I hate smiling!' Jimmy stormed out of the TV studio, glad that another advertisement was finished. It was all part of his master plan. The forced smiles would be worth it when the millions came rolling in.

The owner of the suncream empire drove home, windscreen wipers at full swipe. It certainly wasn't suntan weather but that didn't bother Jimmy. It soon would be. He parked his car and sprinted to his front door, briefcase shielding his face from the rain.

Jimmy lived alone. He had never been a people person. He looked around his tiny apartment. 'I'll soon be upgrading,' he told himself. 'Just as soon as suncream sales take off.'

Jimmy had a plan that was pure evil. He went to the bathroom and looked in the mirror. He saw a handsome man, about thirty years old, with sparkling blue eyes and a mop of black hair. 'See you later, young

Jimmy.' He reached up and grabbed a flap of skin under his chin. There was a squelching sound as he started to peel off his face. Jimmy had spent ten years experimenting with the sun's radiation and it had shrivelled his skin so that he looked as if he'd spent a whole day in the swimming pool. Except Jimmy's wrinkles were deep and sore.

Next came the hair, and his contact lenses came out last. Jimmy fixed his thick-rimmed spectacles on to his face and looked in the mirror again. 'Howdy, old Jimmy.' Thirty had become a hundred and thirty! He'd got used to the red eyes, wrinkly face and burnt scalp. It was the price he'd paid for perfecting his suncream formula.

Jimmy peered at his reflection as he gently stretched his face. 'Ouch,' he yelled. 'Where are my face-ache pills?' He rummaged in the bathroom cabinet and popped a painkiller into his mouth before swigging it down with cold water. Jimmy's evil plan meant sales of his suncream would soon skyrocket. 'Or everyone on the planet will end up looking like me,' he cackled.

★

It was always going to be the most difficult part of her plan. Lara sniffed around the motorway service station, looking for the right opportunity. It was a cold winter's night and many of the lorry drivers had bedded down in their cabs. Others filled their fuel tanks, visited the toilet or bought pasties from the shop.

Lara waited in the shadows. It seemed an age before her chance came. Finally, a lone businessman sat down in the motorway cafe and opened his laptop to check his emails. While the computer was booting up he strolled over to the food counter and started to load up his tray.

I have approximately sixty seconds, thought Lara. *Let's do it!* She jumped through the cafe window and sat at the man's table. It was very late and she was thankful there was nobody around to notice an emailing dog with a rucksack strapped to her back. Lara picked up a teaspoon in her mouth and clicked on to the Internet. She logged in to her email account and tapped a one-line message to Ben, thinking, *The spelling is awful but I'm sure he'll understand*. Lara

clicked Send. The man paid at the till and wandered back to his laptop as the spy dog disappeared into the night.

Lara was hopeful that this would be the last leg of the journey. It had taken two days for her to get this far north. She'd sniffed around the motorway service station and wolfed down a half-eaten burger. *Not enough pickle*, she thought. *I really fancy some pickle. And I'd kill for some chips with mayo.* She looked for a lorry with the right markings. She'd plumped for one with 'Jimmy's Tartan Suncream' emblazoned on the side. *I like the jingle*, she thought. *And Jimmy seems like a nice bloke on the TV ad.*

According to the address on the cab, it

was going to the town where her father lived, so Lara scrambled into the back of the trailer and stowed away with the cargo. She settled down for an uncomfortable night as the wagon trundled out of the service station on its short journey to the Scottish mountains. As Jimmy's lorry ate up the tarmac, the sleeping dog dreamt of chips and mayonnaise.

8. Contact!

The Cook family were very worried. Lara had been gone for two days.

'There's no note or anything,' said Ollie. 'Do you think she's in danger? Could be baddies,' he added, looking concerned.

'Or Mr Big?' suggested Sophie. 'Maybe Lara's arch-enemy has escaped?'

'He's safely behind bars,' explained Dad. 'I'm sure there's some sort of innocent explanation. Has she been acting strangely lately?' he asked in his familiar tell-me-your-secrets voice.

The children were sworn to secrecy but Ollie tried so hard to look innocent that Dad worked out he was guilty. 'What do you know, Ollie?'

'Hardly anything,' blurted the youngest child, unable to resist Dad's special voice. 'I don't know about the diary or anything like that.'

'Shush, stupid,' nudged Sophie.

'What diary?' asked Dad.

'The one that I don't know about,' replied the confused six-year-old.

'Tell me what you don't know,' said Dad, more seriously this time.

Now Ollie was bamboozled. 'Lara's parents. She's been wanting to find out about her mum and dad. She loves us and we love her but she can't help wondering. And we visited an old man in a smelly home and got chased by some people. But we got his diary, Sophie said it was treasure, and Lara read it. But we haven't seen it. We think it tells her about her mum and dad.'

'And where's the diary?' asked Dad calmly.

'We really don't know that, Dad,' explained Ben. 'Lara's kept it private.'

Ben, Sophie and Ollie hunted high and low for the old man's diary but Lara had either kept it well hidden or taken it with her. Ben decided to email his friends to get a search party organized. He noticed one

unread message in his Inbox and clicked to
open it:

*skotland ski place finding dad. Luv u bak
wen hav truth
   lara xxx*

Ben stifled his shout of joy. Instead he
punched the air in delight. 'She's alive and
well . . . and in Scotland.' Ben's energy levels
returned and he did the mad-professor jig.
He could feel an adventure coming on.

Professor Cortex wasn't impressed with Ben's
idea. 'I know where GM451 has gone, and
why. The good news is that she's wearing a
tracking collar so if we can get fairly close
the technology will do the rest. But I can't
just whisk you and your sister and brother
off to Scotland,' he frowned. 'As far as your
mum's concerned, it'd be kidnapping. I'm
already in her bad books, remember?'

Ben and Sophie nodded, recalling their
previous adventures with Lara and the
professor. Mum had shouted at the scientist
last time! The children thought hard about

another idea. 'We have to go and see Lara,' whined Ollie. 'She's all alone and may be in trouble.'

'How about a school skiing holiday?' shouted Ben, alive with an idea. 'There's lots of snow in Scotland at this time of year. We could say that we're going on a school trip and you can come with us cos you're our teacher.'

Sophie and Ollie perked up. It was half an idea.

Professor Cortex removed his spectacles and chewed the ear piece, deep in thought. He was desperate to find GM451 but equally keen to stay in Mrs Cook's good books. 'Ollie's too young,' he said. 'And, besides, fibbing is bad.' The children looked at him expectantly. 'So maybe the truth is better,' he considered. 'I can't risk upsetting your mum again. It's February half-term next week, so maybe your parents will agree to a weekend trip. And if they won't let you come I'll have to go to Scotland alone. Fingers crossed,' smiled the professor.

The children had everything crossed. There was no way they wanted to miss out on this adventure.

9. Much Farther to Father?

Hours later Lara woke as she felt the lorry come to a halt. The back doors creaked open and a man jumped into the back to check the cargo. The spy dog fell completely silent, her ears listening and her nose taking in the smells.

'This is the last batch,' she heard the man call to his colleague. 'Enough emergency suncream for the nation. So we're all set for midweek. It'll be the best fireworks display ever!' Lara heard the two men laughing. 'Let's grab a cuppa and then unload the cargo.'

Lara waited a few minutes before creeping through the boxes and jumping down from the back of the lorry. She was in a massive warehouse. Lara looked around and whistled softly. There were crates of suntan lotion as far as the eye could see. *Thousands! Probably tens of thousands*, she gasped. *This must be the biggest suncream company in the world. I don't know how Jimmy's going to sell all this! He must be praying for some sunshine!*

There were a few warehouse workers around so the dog kept a low profile as she looked for the exit. *My priority is to find my dad*, she thought. *Make contact. Then back home to the kids. They'll be missing me . . . and boy am I missing them!*

Lara nosed through a door and tiptoed down a corridor. *Which way's out?* she thought. She stopped and sniffed. *What on earth's that strange whiff? And this part of the warehouse seems to have people in white coats rather than warehouse workers. It's a bit like spy school.* Lara rounded a corner into another huge warehouse and stopped in amazement. She let out a gasp and sat down in shock. *What kind of business is this?* Lara stared up at the rocket towering above her. *A real space rocket! Wow!* She looked left and right before cautiously sniffing her way around the base of the spacecraft, marvelling at the science and planning that must have gone into building it. She sat and looked up at the red letters on the side of the craft. *OZONE 1.*

It's huge!

The warehouse door began to open and Lara shrank into the background. She watched as a lorry backed into the building and a small army of white-coated men appeared and started milling around.

OK, Lara thought. *This is weird. But all I*

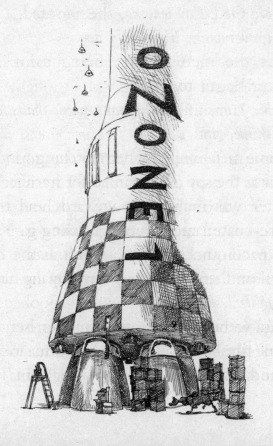

want to do is find my father and go home. Adventure, mystery ... rockets ... it's not my problem.

Lara eyed the warehouse door, now wide open. *That's my way out,* she thought, skulking in the shadows.

But suddenly two of the men saw her and shouted. 'Hey, mutt! Stop that dog!' One of them pressed a button and an alarm sounded.

OK, OK, I'm leaving, she woofed. *Calm down, everybody. It's only a dog.*

But the men weren't being calm. The shutter began to close.

OK, Lara, let the humans panic. Stay calm and think, girl.

Some men jumped at her, clutching handfuls of fur as the spy dog sprinted for her life. The shutter was inching downwards and three white-coated men stood guarding it. *Yikes!* Her pace quickened to a sprint as she bore down on them. *Out of my way. Spy dog coming through!*

Lara went head first into the men, sending them tumbling like skittles. She looked around. *Even more are appearing! And that alarm is deafening.* She looked up to see the shutter three quarters down and falling fast. *Quick or I'm trapped!* Several of the men had picked up large pieces of wood, which they were holding like baseball bats. *Double yikes*, thought Lara, *don't you know I'm supposed to be man's best friend?*

Her heart sank as she spied a man in black uniform carrying a large gun. Lara recognized it from her spy-dog weapons training. *A Taser stun gun!* She shivered. *It shoots bolts of electricity. Not nice!* Lara raised her hackles and issued a warning growl. *This calls for a spy-dog solution.* The man with the Taser was getting scarily close.

Go, Lara, go! Lara ran for her life, zigzagging past the menacing men. One of them brought his wooden baton down hard, narrowly missing Lara but slamming the wood into his mate's head.

Ouch, thought Lara, *that's going to hurt! The shutter is too low. Plan B . . . quick!* Lara spied a yellow forklift truck and jumped aboard, noticing that the keys were in the ignition. She kept her head low as she hit the accelerator, lurching the vehicle forward.

Flooring the pedal she crashed through some wooden boxes. *Which way's out?* she barked as men in white coats leapt out of her path. Taser man was in her way. *No!* she yelped, lurching the vehicle sharply left. Lara heard the buzz of the Taser gun and ducked. Then she heard a man yell as he was accidentally zapped by 3,000 volts of electricity.

The forklift truck hit a large vat of suncream and gallons of the sticky white substance spilt on to the concrete floor. Lara ducked again as a wooden baton splintered against the forklift truck. She heard a lot of yelling as men slipped in the oily liquid. There was no obvious way out so Lara aimed the truck at a door and took the brace position as she crashed through, splintering out into the daylight.

She managed a quick backward glance. There were a dozen men sliding about in the suncream, covered from head to foot. *At least they'll be well protected from the sun.* One man's hair was on end. *He must have been zapped*, she thought. *Sorry, folks. I didn't mean to cause all this confusion. I was just investigating your amazing rocket!*

Lara took in the scene ahead. She was in a huge yard covered in snow and surrounded by barbed wire. *It's like a prison yard*, she thought. *No time to think*. Some of the suncreamed men had slithered to their feet and Taser man was recharging his gun. Lara jumped from the vehicle and grabbed a snow-covered rock. She lumbered back to the truck and climbed aboard, then aimed the truck at the fence and floored the accelerator. The yellow forklift shot forward and Lara did her best to wedge the rock on to the accelerator pedal. *I've seen this on the TV*, she thought. *I just hope it works in real life.*

Lara waited as long as she dared before leaping from the speeding truck and rolling, stuntman-style, through the snow. She looked up to see the truck tangled in the wire. *But there's just enough of a hole*, she spied, *for a dog to escape*. Lara ran, without looking back.

Mum had wobbled a bit before agreeing to the Scotland trip. 'On one condition, Professor,' she'd warned. 'You find Lara and stay put. No action–hero stuff and absolutely no danger.'

Sophie watched the professor twiddling his spectacles nervously. He really was scared of Mum!

'No danger, Mrs Cook. Guaranteed no action–hero stuff, either.'

'And Mr Cook and I will drive up north in three days' time. By then you'll have located Lara and we can enjoy a spot of skiing.'

'Deal,' nodded the professor, mopping his brow. 'Kids, pack your bags, we're going on a dog hunt!'

Lara was exhausted and hungry as she approached the town. *Not far now*, she thought, the butterflies in her stomach flapping like mad. The adventure at the suncream warehouse had been a shock but the thought of seeing her father was even scarier. *What if he's horrible?*

Or if he doesn't want anything to do with me? she thought. *And what if I can't find him? All I know is that he's called Leo and is a mountain rescue dog.*

Lara had cold feet in more ways than one as her snowy paw prints traced a path to the mountain rescue office. The hungry dog raided a bin, scoffing the remains of a tuna sandwich and something that tasted like banana cake. She entered the town and checked out the map at the tourist information centre. The mountain rescue office was clearly marked so she traced her paw to the *You are here* dot. Taking a deep breath she set off to meet her father.

10. Leo the Lyin'

Lara approached the mountain rescue office, heart pounding. It didn't look special; it was more of a Portakabin. *But it might contain someone special. My dad!* she thought as she nosed the door open. *I can't wait to meet him! I wonder what he's like.*

There was nobody around so Lara let herself into the scruffy office. It was nice and warm after the Scottish mountain air. She stood for a minute by the electric fire, toasting her frozen paws. *Ahh, bliss!* Signs of the mountain rescue team were everywhere – ropes looped over hooks, boots lined up on a rack, heavy jackets hanging on pegs. She could smell coffee, so someone must be in there. Lara tiptoed through the first office into the kitchen area – there was a dog sleeping on a rug.

Black and white. Could it be my dad? Do I wake him and ask? Lara was surprised at how nervous she felt. *All those Secret Service missions and I never felt as scared as I do now*, she thought. *How weird.*

Lara noticed the sleeping dog had a collar, so she tiptoed forward, hoping to see if it had 'Leo' written on it. She leant over and squinted as the dog woke with a growl.

'Who are you, mutt? And what are you doin' in my cabin?'

'Er, sorry, sir,' woofed Lara. 'I'm looking for a dog named Leo. Mountain rescue service. Strong as an ox, apparently,' she blurted. 'Do you know him?'

The old dog kept snarling, one ear raised. 'Who's askin'?'

'My name's Lara and I've come a long way to meet him. I've heard he's a real hero. He's rescued loads of people from these mountains.'

The old dog softened and the snarling attitude stopped. 'There was a Leo, a while back,' he barked, 'who was as strong as an ox. But that Leo's gone now. Long gone, lady.'

'It's important that I find him,' declared Lara. 'Where did he go?'

'He just kinda faded away,' replied the old dog. 'Had a tumble on the hills, injured his back legs, which meant he could never be sent to rescue again.'

'Oh dear,' barked Lara. 'And was he a hero?'

The old dog thought for a moment. 'He was brave enough,' he nodded. 'Sometimes too brave. Ya know, he'd take a risk too far.'

Sounds just like me, she smiled. 'Do you know where I can find him?'

'I don't think he wants to be found, lady,'

barked the old dog. 'So, if I were you, I'd back off and go home to wherever you came from. Leo's not interested in meeting ya, whoever ya are.'

'But I only need a minute –'

'I said back off, lady,' growled the old dog, returning to the snarling attitude.

Lara was confused. *There's no need to be unpleasant*, she thought. *But I can see this conversation's going nowhere.* 'OK, I'll leave you in peace,' she woofed as she backed out of the room.

Lara was just leaving the Portakabin as two men entered.

'Cuppa, mate?' asked one.

'Aye,' replied the other.

Lara stood outside the door, ears pricked, as the men entered the kitchen and flicked on the kettle.

'Hi there, Leo, old fella,' said one of the men. 'How are those back legs today?'

Lara's sticky-up ear was at full attention. *Leo?* she thought. *Dad? The old dog, crotchety and miserable. He's my father!*

11. Dangerous Dogs Act

Lara trotted into the nearby town in search of something to eat. She found a fast-food takeaway and rummaged in the bin. *Mmm, there's always a half-eaten burger to be found*, she thought. *Oh, and a few chips.* Lara couldn't work out why she was so hungry. *Must be the Scottish air.*

The retired spy dog wandered the snow-covered streets, thinking hard. As the biting cold wind grew worse, Lara came across a cafe where she could warm up while the thoughts whirred through her mind. Her spy-dog training came as second nature as she waited for the right time, slunk in and found a cosy place under one of the tables. She curled up, exhausted. This was the perfect spy-dog tactic, hidden by the tablecloth but able to peek out whenever she felt the need.

Lara could hear the clinking of knives on plates and chatter of customers. Her ears tuned in to the radio in the background. *That suncream jingle again!* The weather report was grim. *Seems there's a blizzard on the way. I doubt anyone will be wanting Jimmy's Tartan Suncream!*

All she could think about was her father. *I've met him*, she thought. *But he clearly doesn't want anything to do with me, so I'll leave him be. Maybe the professor was right. I could end up doing more harm than good.*

Lara lay with her head on her paws. She was exhausted and her eyelids were drooping. *I'm going home*, she decided, before her eyes closed and she sank into a dream about the best family in the world.

Professor Cortex picked up speed in the Secret Service van. He switched on his special blue flashing light and the traffic miraculously cleared. 'For emergencies only,' he'd winked at the children. 'Except for sometimes when I want to get home for my tea.' The tarmac flashed by as the best family in the world sped towards Scotland.

Lara woke fully refreshed. She peered out from under the tablecloth and waited for the right moment. *I'll just have these sausages, if you don't mind*, she thought, clearing the leftovers from a cooked breakfast. *And a slurp of these beans.* A customer came in and the dog slid out.

Lara trotted back to the warehouse, planning to catch a lorry south. She remembered the men with sticks. *And Taser man! Approach with caution.* The snow was falling more heavily than ever as Lara trudged the four miles back to the warehouse. *It sure seems high security*, she thought, noticing several *Beware of the dogs* signs. *Yikes! I hope there's no trouble this time. I just want a lift home!*

Lara sniffed the air. *Alsatians*, she nodded. *Nice family pets but they can also be trained to be big bad dogs. And what's that funny smell? Like fuel. Maybe gas?* Lara shook her head and refocused. *Stop acting like a spy dog and start being a stowaway dog! I've got a family waiting!*

The barbed-wire fence had been fixed since Lara drove the forklift truck through it, and it now seemed to go on forever before she finally found a small gap and wriggled through. She got her backpack caught on the wire and was trapped half in and half out of the compound.

Ouch! she whined as she tried to reverse.

'Ouch, indeed,' growled a large black guard dog. 'How unlucky to be caught trying to break into our territory.'

Lara's heart sank. 'OK, guys,' she began. 'I'm sorry for breaking in but I'm just after a lift home in one of your lorries. Perhaps you can help?'

The Alsatians howled with laughter. 'We're guard dogs, lady, not guide dogs,' said one.

'And we don't help . . . we hurt!' snarled the other. 'Especially when we've caught you breaking in.'

Lara sighed. *It's certainly not an ideal situation,* she thought. *I've tackled big dogs before, and won. But these are very big dogs . . . trained to hurt . . . and I'm hooked on this fence. Think, Lara, think.*

The biggest dog raised his hackles and

approached the trapped spy dog. He lashed out a paw and caught her across the shoulder, drawing blood. 'We don't like intruders, do we, Blaze?'

'No, Bullet. Our mission is to seek and destroy,' snarled his companion. 'We're police dogs see, gone wrong!'

'Police dogs, eh?' barked Lara, calm on the outside but panicking on the inside. 'I guess I shouldn't hurt you too badly, then,' she snapped, wriggling to free herself from the barbs. Lara didn't have time for these bullies.

'Doesn't look like you're in a position to hurt anybody,' growled Bullet, curling his lip to reveal some brilliant white fangs. He sprang at Lara just as she released the clip from her backpack. Bullet attacked the bag, gripping it in his teeth and shaking it from side to side. But Lara was gone. He dropped the backpack at his feet and turned to see Lara dancing about on her hind legs, karate-style. The guard dogs turned to each other, a little confused.

Lara did a kick and punch into the air. 'OK, fellas, bring it on,' she barked. Her

hackles were raised in an attempt to look as big and threatening as she could. *I'm a black belt*, she thought, *but these are a pair of snarling brutes.* Both of her attackers crouched low, teeth bared, ready to pounce.

Yikes, thought Lara, still dancing. *They're like wolves! This is scary!*

Bullet came at her again in a flurry of teeth and claws. She felt the scratch marks in her shoulder as she punched with all her might. She landed a terrific blow and the dog yelped in pain.

Blaze was coming next. Lara swung her leg and kicked him in the belly, while landing a decent blow on Bullet's nose. The attacking dogs were down but not out. They regrouped, blood streaming from their noses and mouths. Bullet spat a tooth out.

Blaze's eyes were watering. 'Now you've made me really angry,' he barked in a high-pitched tone.

Lara was worried. *These are seriously hard dogs! Remember your training, Lara. Sometimes it's best to avoid a fight.* She spotted an open door to the warehouse up ahead and decided to go for it.

The bully dogs pounced again and Lara ran for her life, yanking her backpack from the wire on the way as she put her tail and ears down to ease wind resistance. *Can't forget my gadgets*, she thought to herself. The Alsatians were after her, but with a head start she made it through the door and slammed it behind her, hoping they wouldn't get through. She heard wild barking and scratching as they threw themselves at the closed door.

Too much noise, she worried. *I must get them to shut up.* Lara dumped her rucksack on the floor and looked around the room. *It's a staff kitchen.* She took a deep breath and worked out a plan as the fierce barking continued outside.

Ten seconds later Lara jumped and opened the door. A pair of very angry Alsatians bounded through. But Lara was prepared. She hit Bullet with a frying pan and, *bang*, he was out cold. Blaze came at her and Lara picked up a chair to fend him off.

'Down, boy,' she urged. 'Settle yourself.'

But Blaze wasn't for settling. He was in attack mode so Lara had no choice but to defeat him. Twenty seconds later the unconscious dogs lay side by side.

Who'd have thought a wooden spoon would be so effective? she thought. It didn't look like a useful weapon but Lara knew exactly where to aim and the hollow sound as it hit Blaze's head had made a strangely satisfying *clonk*.

Phew, gasped Lara. *That was a bit chaotic. I'd best get out of here quickly!* She nosed her way out of the kitchen, into a corridor and sniffed again. *Which way for a lorry? And what is that strange smell again?* she wondered. *It's getting stronger.*

Lara heard the *beep beep* of a lorry reversing. *That's my ticket home*, she thought. The retired spy dog bounded down the hallway to peer through the warehouse door. *What's going on?* she asked herself as she watched the scene unfold in front of her.

The *beep beep* was a lorry all right. It had reversed into a loading bay and OZONE 1 was being lifted on to the back of the truck. Lara watched as the rocket was laid flat and covered up. *How strange. This is a suntan-lotion factory, and it's producing rockets. I just don't get it.*

Lara observed for a few minutes more as the rocket was secured and the lorry pulled away. She was torn. *The pull of my family is one thing . . . but a rocket?* she thought, cocking her head in consideration. *And a strange smell of gas? I reckon it's worth investigating. Just for a moment, anyway.*

Lara bounded up the fire escape stairs and let herself into the warehouse. *Once a spy dog, always a spy dog!*

12. Space Age

The professor was getting excited as the van sped past the *Welcome to Scotland* sign. The receiver in Sophie's hand lit up, a tiny dot bleeping away. 'That's her,' he explained to the children. 'We're within range. Find that dot and we find GM451.'

The warehouse was full of men in white coats. *And why such high security for a suncream factory? Something fishy's going on. Let's see what I can sniff out.* Lara followed her nose, tail wagging excitedly. Her sniffing took her to a large tank, shaped like an oil drum, with all sorts of hazard signs stuck to the side. *Clearly a dangerous gas*, she thought, shying away from the strong odour. A nearby door flew open and Lara shrank into a corner as a pair of men stepped out of an office. She strained to listen ... *I half recognize that voice.*

'So just one tank of superconcentrated CFC gas left to fill,' she heard. 'And then we load it on to the rocket and hey presto!' The men chuckled together.

'A big fireworks display for the whole of Scotland,' laughed one of the men as they hurried by.

That voice, she thought. *It's Jimmy off the suncream ads. Maybe I can get his autograph for the kids?* Lara emerged from the dark corner, annoyed that she couldn't fit the pieces of the jigsaw together. *Maybe I should check out the office where the men have come from.* Lara jumped up on to her hind legs and pulled at the office door. She padded in, sniffing the air, ears on full alert. *Files, laptops ... normal office stuff.* Lara cocked her head and listened. She heard the men approaching the office again and made a dash for the curtains.

Yikes, they're too short, I can't hide there ... Under the desk? ... Too obvious ... The filing cabinet, it's my only chance. Lara tugged at the metal handle and the bottom drawer slid out.

Aaah, it's full of files. She banged it shut, the footsteps getting nearer. The next draw was half full. *No chance.* She stood on tiptoes and pulled at the top drawer. *Empty. Brilliant.*

The men were about to enter the room. Lara leapt on to the desk and sent a lamp crashing to the floor. *Whoops!* In one impressive bound, she was inside the filing cabinet. The drawer glided shut and Lara lay hidden in the cramped darkness.

The men heard the crash as they swung open the office door. 'What was that?' shouted Jimmy. 'Who's there?'

'The lamp's fallen, somehow,' said his colleague, picking up some of the pieces.

Jimmy put his finger to his lips and picked up the broken lamp. 'An intruder,' he mouthed. He checked under the desk before pointing to the curtains. It was the only other hiding place. Jimmy held the broken lamp high while his colleague tiptoed to the window and tore the curtains apart.

'Nobody,' gasped his mate, puffing out his cheeks in relief. 'It must have been a gust of wind.'

'Agreed,' said Jimmy, lowering the lamp. 'I

guess we're both a bit jumpy. We're so close to pulling off the biggest plot since Guy Fawkes! Let's get on with the meeting.'

The spy dog crouched in the dark of the top drawer, listening to the muffled conversation. *It's so uncomfortable,* she thought, *with my hind leg behind my ear! I hope the guys are quick!*

'I'm filming one more set of advertisements tonight,' said Jimmy. 'Our ads will be beamed to every home in the land twenty times a day until everyone's singing our blasted jingle.'

'Excellent,' nodded his colleague. 'Then all we need are harmful rays ... lots of harmful rays! So let's go through the schedule one more time,' Lara heard the muffled voice say. 'The rocket is already on its way to Ben

Nevis. We've secured a launch site near the top of the mountain.'

'Good,' said Jimmy. 'And we're filling the final CFC gas tank as we speak. That's to be transported tonight and fixed to the rocket first thing.'

Lara grimaced in pain as she strained to hear. 'And then, the best bit,' she heard. 'Tomorrow we launch the rocket and time it to explode in the Earth's ozone layer and destroy it. *Caboom!*' laughed the man. 'A free fireworks display!'

'So no more ozone layer above Scotland,' snarled Jimmy.

'Which is sad for everyone else, but not for us. All that radiation is allowed to beam down to Earth and there's only one way to protect yourself.'

'Jimmy's Tartan Suncream,' chorused the men together, breaking into the jingle once more. 'They'll be queuing round the block. We're gonna make millions. Billions, even!'

'Prove the technology works and then we go global, punching holes in the ozone layer above major cities all over the world,' said Jimmy's colleague.

Jimmy's face grinned as widely as the plastic face mask would allow. Global domination was his favourite hobby.

Lara was desperate on two fronts. On the one hand she now knew the plan and needed to escape to stop the rocket. *It's an evil scheme*, she thought. *Jolly Jimmy is really Deadly Jimmy! If they launch the rocket there will be an environmental disaster.*

But Lara had a priority that, at that moment, was even more urgent than saving the world. *I've got cramp in my leg. And it's killing me. Aargh, the pain!* Lara pulled a wonky doggie face and bit her tongue in an attempt not to howl. But it was so bad that in the end she had no choice.

Rat-a-tat-tat. Lara tapped on the metal door with her claw. *Er, hello, guys*, came the muffled yelp. *Can someone let me out? Please? I'm stuffed in here like an oven-ready chicken!*

The men went quiet, exchanging glances and looking at the cabinet.

'Is that an animal?' said the other man.

Jimmy reached for a drawer and pulled out a Taser gun. He switched it on and Lara heard the familiar buzz as it charged. 'I have no idea, but you open it,' he mouthed, 'and I'll get it.'

Lara was now hurting badly but she could hear the Taser gun charging up and she knew she was in trouble when the drawer opened. *Too late now, unfortunately!* Lara figured her only chance of escape was to surprise Jimmy and his evil friend. *And with a stun gun pointing at me, it will have to be a big surprise!*

Jimmy's sidekick hauled open the sliding drawer and Lara sprang like a jack-in-the-

box, uncoiled and free. A bolt of electricity zapped at the blur of fur as it sped by. Lara was away, sprinting down the corridor as fast as her backpack would allow. *It's so good to be free!* She took corners at top speed, imagining angry dogs and men with Taser guns beginning to take chase. Lara bolted across the snowy courtyard, looking out for angry Alsatians, then charged through the hole in the wire fence and didn't stop until she was almost back in town. Her chest heaved in and out and her muscles ached.

But at least I've escaped, she thought, looking back to check there was nobody following. *All I have to do now is find the rocket and defuse the bomb!*

Lara trotted past a giant poster advertising Jimmy's Tartan Suncream and shuddered at his evil grin. *The future of the planet is in my paws. I have less than twenty-four hours to stop the rocket*, she groaned. *Or Scotland and then the whole world fries!*

13. Rendezvous

Ben, Sophie, Ollie and the professor stepped out of the van and stretched their weary limbs. Ollie couldn't resist bending down to pick up a handful of snow, which was immediately moulded into a snowball and thrown at his big brother. Professor Cortex wasn't in the mood and one of his stern looks was enough for Ben to drop his own snowball.

'Ladies and gentlemen,' he pleaded, 'we are here on important business. Your pet and my beloved spy dog is somewhere very close. I suggest we get started on the search.'

Sophie handed him the receiver and all eyes fell on the red dot. 'Well, well. It appears she's coming our way!'

Ollie was the first to see her in the distance. Sophie started sprinting, Ben quickly overtaking her. By the time the professor caught up, Lara was being lovingly hugged by three children.

'What have you done to your side, Lara?' asked Ollie. 'You're bleeding.'

Oh, you know, baddies, evil plots, rockets, poisonous gas, electric guns, barbed wire . . . the usual spy-dog stuff.

'Good afternoon, GM451,' said the professor matter-of-factly. 'I trust you've found what, or who, you were looking for?'

Lara nodded, looking sad. *Yeah, I found my dad, Prof. Mr Jetski's diary was right. He's not exactly the hero I'd expected, though.*

'And I'm sure he's a handsome hero,' smiled the professor. 'But now your curiosity's satisfied, I'm hoping you want to return home with your family.'

I'd like nothing more, thought Lara. *But we have to save the planet first! How do I fill you in on the adventure? Maybe a mime? It's worked before.* Lara shrugged the children off and waved her paws for calm. *OK*, she woofed. *Here goes . . .*

The children watched in shock as their

dog went through a bizarre series of arm movements, acting out a rocket lift-off, before ending in a fantastic *caboom* sequence that Oscar-winning actors would have been proud of. She staggered around, clutching her throat.

And we all suffer from poisonous rays from the sun, she wailed, jabbing her paw at the sky. *And then, we rub suntan cream all over our bodies, like this,* she demonstrated. Lara started to whistle the jingle from Jimmy's Tartan Suncream advert, until all the children were grinning and singing along. *So we catch the baddies,* she mimed, doing a few karate moves, *get Jimmy locked up and save the planet. And that completes my doggie mime. Ta daaa!* Lara did a dainty curtsy and looked hopefully at her owners. *Got it?*

The professor was scratching his bald head. Ben was shaking his. Sophie's eyebrows were deep in thought.

'There's a message in there somewhere,' she noted. 'Someone's been strangled? And you're rubbing yourself because of the cold?'

'And there's some karate,' offered Ollie enthusiastically.

'And Jimmy saves the day?' guessed Ben.

Lara clasped her head in her paws. *This is so frustrating! He doesn't save the day, he destroys the planet!*

'Prof, go and get your laptop and let's get Lara to type it out,' suggested Ollie.

Nice thinking, young chap, barked Lara, high-fiving Ollie. *Sometimes it takes the six-year-old to come up with the best solution.*

The party went to Lara's favourite cafe, ordered five huge meals and watched as the family pet tapped away with a pencil in her mouth. Lara looked at her handiwork. *Not bad for a dog,* she thought.

Sophie read the paragraph out loud, stumbling over some of the spellings:

Baddies launch rocket tuesday. Big bang OF cfcgas. OZONe hole lets rays thru. Bad sunburn unless you buy sunCREME. Eviil plot. Needs stopinG. JimmMMY is EVIL. And I fancy 2x salami and bANANa pizza.

'No way,' gasped Ollie, 'not salami and banana!'

'That's not the important bit, silly,' said Sophie. 'It says Jimmy's behind an evil plan. I can't believe it! Jimmy seems like a really nice man. His advert is dead funny.'

Yeah, well, what he's about to do to the ozone layer isn't very funny, thought Lara gravely. *But 'dead' just about sums it up!*

'Tuesday?' yelled Ben. 'That's tomorrow!'

Well done, Sherlock, nodded Lara. *So we need to work quickly. And don't forget the last sentence. Salami and banana, please. Times two. My tummy's rumbling.*

'Where is the rocket taking off from, GM451?' asked the professor.

Near Topp OF BEn Nevisssss, came the typed reply.

'And what's CFC gas?' asked Ollie.

Professor Cortex looked over the top of his spectacles and adopted his serious voice. 'CFCs are gases found in things like spray cans and fridges. Governments have tried to reduce them because they damage part of the atmosphere that we call the ozone layer. And GM451's right, it's the ozone layer that protects us from the sun's most harmful rays.'

'So launching CFC gas into the ozone layer is definitely a bad thing, then?' asked Sophie.

'I'm doing global warming for my project,' noted Ben. 'Bad is an understatement!'

'It would be a catastrophe for the planet,' sighed the professor. 'It's evil beyond imagination.' He continued peering at them over the top of his specs. 'Without the ozone layer there's no filter. The full power of the sun's rays would inflict a great deal of damage to our skin.'

'So we'd all have to buy Jimmy's suncream!' piped up Sophie. '*That*'s his evil scheme.'

Professor Cortex turned his full attention to Lara. 'You say the rocket has already been transported. What about the gas canisters? Have they gone up the mountain yet?'

Lara took the pencil in her mouth once more and everyone stared as the characters appeared on the laptop screen.

2NITE. 'Tonight!' gasped the professor. 'So no time to lose. Then I suggest we follow the shipment of gas, find the rocket and stop it before launch.'

A smiley face appeared on-screen and Lara gave the thumbs-up sign. *And after we've saved the world we can all go home and live happily ever after!*

'Good work, GM451,' nodded the professor. 'Even though you're retired this is a very serious case.' He called over to the waitress. 'Can I order an extra large banana and salami pizza, please?'

X2 appeared on the screen.

'Two of them, please,' asked the professor, casting a your-eyes-are-bigger-than-your-belly look at GM451.

WITH maYo appeared on the screen.

'Well really, GM451!' sighed Professor Cortex. 'What bad eating habits you've got into.'

Lara licked her lips. *I'm so hungry*, she thought. *I might even try haggis!*

14. Stowaway Kids

The professor followed Lara's directions and parked his van a discreet distance from the barbed-wire fence. Lara took the binoculars and scanned the scene. She could see the Alsatians patrolling and thought it wise to keep a safe distance between them and the children. She bounded on top of the van and took a closer look. Through the binoculars' magnified vision she could make out three large canisters being loaded into a lorry. The tailgate was shut and the driver jumped in. A barrier was raised and the truck started driving in their direction.

Quick, everyone! Action stations! I need to get into the back of that vehicle, she thought. *My guess is that those canisters are heading for the rocket launch site. Someone needs to create a diversion.*

Everyone looked at Lara, confused. 'What's all the excitement about, Lara?' asked Sophie.

The next vehicle coming down this road. I need to be stowed away in the back. Got it?

'Calm down, GM451,' said the professor. 'What's going on? What have you seen? Is it the baddies?'

Lara nodded. *No time to think. Here goes.* Lara mimed her best driving skills, her paws gripping an imaginary steering wheel. *Lorry coming. Please understand.*

'Milking a cow?' suggested Sophie.

Lara looked at the children in despair. *OK, no more mimes. This is where I take control!* Lara led the children out of sight behind a bush before returning to the professor's van and letting one of the tyres down.

'Hey,' he shouted above the hiss, 'what on earth are you doing to my van?'

Pretend you need help, barked Lara. *Flag down the lorry, create a diversion and I'll hop into the back with the gas bottles.*

The professor was left confused as Lara joined the children behind the bush. He stood in the road, scratching his head. A lorry crawled round the corner from the direction of the warehouse. 'I hope this is what you want me to do, GM451,' he said as he raised his hands for it to stop. 'Evening, gentlemen,' he said as the driver's window slid down. 'I'm having tyre trouble and I was wondering if you could give me a hand?'

Lara crept to the back of the truck and beckoned for the children to follow. *I need help to lower the tailgate,* she thought. *And to close it after I'm safely aboard.*

From the corner of his eye, the professor saw the children and Lara sneak out of their hiding place. He realized what was happening and tried to stall for time. 'I don't want to be stuck here in the bad weather,' he complained, pointing at the heavens.

'Not our problem, old man,' said the unhelpful driver.

Ben had quietly lifted the tailgate and Lara was about to jump in.

'And we're on a tight schedule,' shouted the passenger. 'We have a special delivery.'

As Ben bent down to help Lara into the back of the vehicle his mobile phone dropped from his pocket and clattered on to the icy tarmac. The children froze.

The professor upped his level of chattiness, hoping the men hadn't heard the noise. 'Tyre as flat as a pancake,' he gabbled. 'And do you know, I've not had a pancake since America in '67. Or was it '68? Maple syrup if I recall . . .'

The man in the passenger seat had heard the noise and began to get suspicious. He opened his door and looked behind. 'What was that?' he said. 'You get rid of the pensioner and I'll check the cargo.'

Yikes! thought Lara.

Ben, Sophie and Ollie looked at her with terrified eyes. 'What are we going to do?' mouthed Sophie. 'Where can we hide?'

Lara looked round, panicking slightly. *These guys are dangerous*, she thought, remembering the Taser gun. *I've got five seconds to hide the kids! There's only one place!* Lara pushed the children into the back of the lorry and Ben put the tailgate in place. The man came round to the back of the vehicle and Lara knew it was too late for her to hide. *Just act like a normal dog*, she thought, cocking her leg up against the wheel.

'Just a pesky mutt,' the man shouted, kicking out at Lara. 'Stop piddling on my car! Scoot!' he yelled.

The man returned to his seat and slammed the door angrily. He signalled the driver to go. Lara watched in horror as the lorry lumbered away with the three Cook children stowed in the back.

Whoops, that wasn't supposed to happen!

Lara gave chase, spurred on by Sophie's panicked face peering out of the back of the lorry. *I can't keep up*, she puffed as the lorry sped off. *But don't worry, kids. I'll think of something.*

Lara sloped back to the professor. 'Where are the children?' he asked, looking for them behind the bush.

Er, you're not going to like this, Prof, wheezed Lara, her sticky-up ear drooping to half mast.

'GM451, *where are the children?*' barked the professor, louder this time. The spy dog's body language said it all. 'What?' he shouted, watching the truck disappear into the mountains. 'You hid them in the back of the van? With some canisters of poisonous gas? Heading for a rocket launch site? In a blizzard?'

Er, I said you wouldn't like it, whimpered Lara, shrugging her doggie shoulders.

'This is worse than terrible,' spat the professor. 'It's downright awful.'

Even worse, cringed Lara, *we've got a flat tyre so we can't chase them! But don't worry, Prof. I'll come up with a plan.*

One man and his spy dog strode quickly towards the town. Professor Cortex was wondering whether 'awful' was really worse than 'terrible'. His dog knew that both words were equally bad.

'What will I say to Mrs Cook if she phones, GM451? We have to get the children back to safety immediately,' said the professor.

Sometimes things don't go quite according to plan, thought Lara, frantically working out how to rescue the children from the very dangerous situation she'd got them into.

15. Climbing Solo

The walk into town had exhausted the professor. 'I'll check into a hotel and see if I can hire a four-wheel drive,' he explained. 'And you, GM451, why not have a sniff around town while we wait. See if you can find some clues.'

Dusk had brought a storm and the streets were quiet as snow swirled around the street lamps. Lara looked up at the mountains and thought of the children. *I have to find them. I can't wait for the professor and his truck. The children are in danger and I know someone with the skills to help me.*

The old dog was just leaving the mountain rescue Portakabin as Lara approached.

'Leo,' she barked. 'I need your help urgently.'

'You again,' he woofed, looking surprised. 'How do you know my name? Anyway, I thought I told you "Leo" wasn't interested?'

'But I need you to help me on a mission,' pleaded Lara. 'And to be a real hero.'

Her father barked a doggie laugh. 'With these legs?' he said, limping towards his owner's car. "Hero Leo" is well and truly retired, seeing his days out by the fire. Even if I wanted to help ... which I don't ... then I couldn't.'

'What if I told you there were some

children trapped on the mountain?' begged Lara. 'And I love them. You must have children ... puppies ... that you love?'

Leo fell silent, remembering the litter of puppies from a couple of years ago. 'Aye,' he barked, 'my lady and I had some pups, a while back. Gorgeous creatures. Black and white, clever like their ma. But she and they were taken away. I'm told they were all special ... but not me, girl. I'm not special. Just a normal hound. An old one at that.'

'Come on, Leo,' called his owner. 'Time to go home, old fella. There's a blizzard brewing so no one's daft enough to go up the mountains tonight. Pity them if they do.'

Lara looked at her father. 'You are special, Leo,' she barked. 'I know you are. Please? I need a guide – someone who knows the mountains like the back of their paw. One last mission?'

Leo's owner picked up the heavy dog and heaved him into the passenger seat.

He's too old even to jump up, Lara thought. *I guess it's unfair to ask.*

'I'd fear for anyone in the mountains

tonight,' he barked. 'Big storm brewin'. It's too dangerous, lady. You should go home.'

The car door slammed shut and Leo was driven away. Lara chased the car for a few hundred metres.

This is desperate, she thought as she gave up, panting heavily. *I'll never find the launch site by myself. But I just can't let the children down*, she thought through doggie tears. A car drove by and snowy slush splashed in her face. *I got Ben, Sophie and Ollie into this mess, and it's up to me to get them out of it!*

Lara tightened her rucksack strap and set off towards the mountains, following the signs towards Ben Nevis. The swirling snow had been replaced by a driving blizzard and she squinted into the eye of the storm. *This is going to be my most difficult mission yet!*

16. Proud

Ben, Sophie and Ollie crouched in the back of the truck, too terrified to talk or move. They could feel themselves being dragged up and up the mountain, round lots of very sharp bends, as the vehicle clung to the road. It was well after dark when the vehicle stopped and the men got out. A head poked into the back and a torch shone into the darkness. The children lay still, curled up under a canvas tarpaulin.

'At first light, we fix these canisters to the rocket,' said one. 'But let's get some kip first. Tomorrow is going to be a long day.'

The children heard footsteps trudge through the snow, until the only sound was the howling wind buffeting the lorry.

Ben poked his head out into the darkness

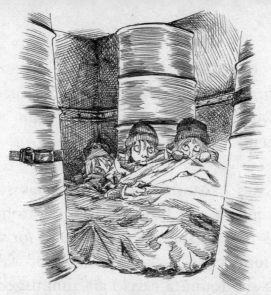

and felt the force of the storm blowing into his face. 'There's nothing except snow,' he said. 'It's a real blizzard. We're going to have to stay in here for the night.' He pulled at the key ring the professor had given him for Christmas and shone the small torch around the back of the wagon. They were stowed away with three large canisters, a bit like oil drums. In the corner was a bag containing warm outdoor coats and the children put them on and snuggled up, pulling the canvas sheet back over them like a tent. Ollie's instant snoring provided some comfort to the older children.

'Is Lara going to rescue us?' whispered Sophie in the darkness.

'Let's get some sleep,' said Ben, squeezing her hand. 'I'm sure Lara and the professor are working on a plan right at this very moment.'

Lara was exhausted. The climb was steep and slippery and the wind was so strong it felt as though she took three steps forward and four steps back. Darkness had fallen when she found a cave. Lara rummaged in her rucksack and found her arctic suit.

Yes, it looks silly, she thought, *but this is a life or death situation. And besides, nobody will see me up here at night.* The spy dog pulled on the clinging Lycra suit and was transformed into a Superdog lookalike. *Mmm, I feel warmer already.* She removed a torch helmet from her bag and fixed it to her head. She thought of the children being taken away in the lorry. *No time to lose. Sleep is not an option.*

Lara stepped out into the biting wind, her torch lighting the way as she trudged onwards into the dark.

Professor Cortex had made several frantic phone calls trying to get hold of a four-wheel drive vehicle. He'd phoned the Secret Service and ordered a fleet of agents to Jimmy's warehouse, but with the roads closed they couldn't get a four-wheel drive to him for another few hours, and the mountain rescue office was closed overnight. He paced up and down the hotel room, waiting for daylight to come.

'There's not much more I can do,' he told himself as he sank into a chair and flicked on the news. He sighed at the weather report. 'Stupid woman,' he muttered as the chirpy presenter announced that the worst blizzard to hit Scotland in twenty years had brought great news for skiers and snowboarders.

'But not for kidnapped children,' he complained to the TV. He wondered about GM451. 'She's been gone a long while,' he told himself. The old man settled into his chair. The TV droned on. It was dark outside and his eyes felt heavy. The professor's eyelids fought against it, but after a long drive and a tough walk through the snow, he finally lost the war against sleep.

★

After a restless night, dawn came and the children awoke. Ben peered out of the back of the lorry and gasped at the scenery. 'The blizzard's almost stopped,' he croaked. 'There's clear sky over there.'

Ollie was desperate for a wee so the boys slipped out and wrote their names in the snow.

'We're near the top of a mountain,' whispered Ben to his brother. 'And get a load of that!' he gasped, finger pointing at a rocket, standing tall against the whiteness of the snow.

'Wow!' gasped Ollie. It's like *Thunderbird 3*! What's it for?'

'That must be the rocket Lara told us about,' explained Ben. 'The canisters of gas are going to be bolted on and it'll be launched today.'

'Wow!' repeated Ollie. 'Into space!'

'And, do you know what?' added Ben. 'We're the only ones who can stop them! It's a race against time.'

'Wow!' whispered Ollie, claiming a hat-trick. 'A space race! What about Lara? Shouldn't we wait for her?'

'Yes,' said Sophie, sneaking up beside them. 'And Professor Cortex will be going crazy. Let's not do anything stupid.'

'Well, they're not here, silly. I think it's our turn to solve something for once,' Ben instructed. 'We know how important this is.'

'But –' started Sophie.

'Shhhhh,' Ben warned suddenly, grabbing Sophie and Ollie and ducking down. 'There are lights in that cabin. I think the men are up and about. Let's scoot.'

The sun's first rays crept over the horizon and Lara was still climbing. *It's a bit easier in*

the light, she thought, *but I don't even know if I'm heading the right way.* Lara stopped for a rest and a think. She rummaged in her rucksack for something to eat. *Mmm, a bar of chocolate*, she thought, tearing off the silver paper and gobbling it down.

'I'll be needing half of that, lady,' bellowed a voice. 'And this is no time to rest, not if there are kids to be rescued.'

'Leo!' barked Lara, as she watched the old dog struggle up the hill. 'You've made it. How on earth did you find me?'

'The back legs might be on their way out,' grinned the old dog, 'but the nose is in perfect working order.'

'You're going to help me. You *are* a hero!'

'Not a hero, lady,' he said. 'But there's summat about you I like. You remind me of myself. And what's an old dog to do when he's told there's one last mission?' Lara noticed a spark in her father's eye. He sat awkwardly, his ageing legs clearly not up to the journey. 'Now, where are we going, exactly?'

Lara quickly explained the whole story. 'There's a rocket . . . and some baddies . . . and some dangerous gas . . . and it's going to destroy the ozone layer . . . and then they make millions from selling their suncream . . . so basically we're all in big trouble!'

'Slow down, girl,' he said. 'Why are you wearing your pyjamas and what's yer name?'

'Oh, it's a special suit to keep out the cold. I know it looks silly. And I'm Lara,' she said, holding out her leg and shaking her dad warmly by the paw.

'Lovely name,' he smiled. 'Righty ho, Lara. Let's keep calm. A rocket will have to be launched from a relatively flat spot. Right?'

'Right.'

'And there's only one flat spot in this neck of the woods. The east side of Ben Nevis. Thataway,' pointed the old dog, towards an even higher peak.

'How far?' asked Lara.

'Ten, maybe twelve miles?' guessed Leo. 'Are you up for it?'

'Sure am, Da— I mean, Leo,' smiled Lara.

The two dogs marched onwards and upwards, their doggie footprints soon covered by fresh snow.

17. Tug of Life

The blizzard's wind had died down but the snow was still falling as the two dogs struggled up the mountain. Lara had looped some rope through their collars so they were tied together.

'I saw it in a film once. If one of us falls, the other one can save them,' she'd shouted above the gale. It also meant she could pull her dad up the really steep sections. Lara breathed a sigh of relief as she came to a flat section. 'An easy bit,' she called back.

But as Lara stepped on to the smooth surface, her foot went straight through the ice. She howled with terror as her body fell into a deep crevasse and she was left dangling on the end of the rope, her collar strangling her.

'Help!' she panted, her legs flailing wildly. 'Help me!'

Leo was some way back, eyes squinting into the wind, concentrating on one step at a time. As Lara fell he was suddenly dragged along by the rope, his claws scratching for a hold. Leo's tired back legs finally found some grip and he sat in the snow, the rope clutched in his mouth. He leant back, tug-of-war style, taking the strain of the rope. He couldn't see Lara but knew she was in trouble.

'Don't worry, Lara,' he woofed out of the corner of his mouth. 'I'll haul you out.'

Little by little, Lara felt her body being winched upwards. She was powerless to help, swinging by her collar in the ice cave. Her bulging eyes looked around and the flashlight on her head pointed down into the crevasse. *Just a sheer drop into the darkness. If my dad lets go, it's certain death.*

Leo was pulling with all his might, inching backwards.

I'm being strangled, Lara spluttered. She could see the hole above. *I wish I hadn't eaten that second pizza*, she thought. *Keep going,*

*Dad. I know you must be
exhausted but please keep going.*

Leo's back legs were wobbling,
his muscles aching and lungs
bursting. It wasn't a tug-of-war,
it was a tug-of-life! Lara reached
up and grasped the icy ledge with
her front paws.

'Come on, Dad. One more
heave,' she gasped, not caring
if he heard her.

One more heave was all Leo could
muster. Lara scrambled from the ice hole as
her dad collapsed in a heap. Lara ran to
him.

'That's me done, Lara,' he gasped. 'This
old dog's done for.'

Lara looked down at her dad, collapsed
in the snow. *He's such a hero to have come this
far*, she thought. *And to have saved my life.
I'm so proud.*

'OK,' she barked. 'But the clearing is just

over the next hill. I have to go on alone. Here,' she woofed, 'take this collar. It has a special tracking device so I'll be able to come back and get you later. And put this suit on,' she added, wriggling out of her Lycra outfit. 'It'll be much warmer and you've earned it – superhero!'

Leo staggered to his feet and Lara used her teeth to pull the Lycra suit over him. He slumped to the ground under a rocky ledge and closed his eyes, overcome with exhaustion. 'You go on ahead, Lara. The old fella just needs some rest. Come back for me later.'

Lara gave her dad a loving nuzzle as the professor's special suit started to warm him up. But there was no time to waste, and so she finally charged on, leaving her father to recover. She looked at him from a distance. *Be safe, Dad.*

She was exhausted and starving. The wind chill was making her teeth chatter. Her face was white and there was an icicle forming on the end of her nose. She looked over the edge of the ridge, sheer drops either side. *One slip and I'm a goner*, she thought. Ears flat to her head, Lara inched forward, getting closer to the children with every step.

Ben, Sophie and Ollie found a safe spot where they could see everything. They watched as three other men unloaded the large drums from the back of the lorry. They rolled them over to the rocket and used a winch to lift them into position.

'Look,' whispered Ben. 'Lara's right – that is Jimmy from the suncream adverts!'

'Hold steady,' shouted the driver, 'and I'll bolt the first gas bottle into place.'

It took the men most of the morning. While they were all out working, Sophie sneaked into the cabin and stole a packet of biscuits and a bottle of juice, returning with her breakfast treasure. She looked scared as she handed over the snacks.

'Are you OK?' asked Ben through a mouthful of biscuits.

'They've . . . they've . . . they've got guns in there!' exclaimed Sophie, her eyes wide with fear.

Ben and Ollie stopped mid-crunch, eyes wide in horror.

'I sooo wish Lara was here,' wailed Ollie. 'She'd know what to do.'

'Well, she's not,' said Ben bravely. 'It's up to us to come up with a plan. Simple as that.'

Professor Cortex was woken by his mobile phone. He surprised Mrs Cook with his startled manner. 'Yes, what, who?' he spluttered in a half-asleep state. 'Ah, Mrs Cook,' he said, looking quickly around the room to remind himself where he was. He couldn't believe it was the morning. 'Good to hear from you. You're on your way up here! Splendid,' he lied. The professor's brow creased as he listened to Mrs Cook's next question. 'How are the kids?' he repeated. The professor hated

lying, partly because he was very bad at it. 'Having the adventure of a lifetime,' he said, avoiding a fib.

'And *where* are the children?' asked Mrs Cook. 'Can I have a quick word with them?'

'They've popped out,' blurted the professor. 'On a mission ... I mean an errand,' he stammered, slapping his forehead in frustration at his poor answer.

'At this time of the morning? Are the children OK?' asked Mum suspiciously.

'OK?' repeated the professor. 'Why do you ask that?'

'Oh, you know,' added Mum, much more sternly, 'you've been in a few scrapes in the past. Guns, diamonds, robberies. So you can't blame me for checking if they're safe.'

'Safe?' laughed the professor, struggling for anything other than a complete lie. 'As in "protected from harm"?'

'Yes, Professor, as in "protected from harm",' replied Mum, her tone ever more serious.

'All I can say, Mrs C, is that the children are having a terrific adventure.' The professor mopped his brow. 'Erm, sorry, but I'm losing the signal. There's nothing to worry about,' he blurted before snapping his mobile shut and dabbing his brow once more. 'Except rockets, poisonous gas and evil men who want to destroy the planet!' he added, gasping for breath and reaching for his blood-pressure pills.

The professor took a deep breath and held it a while. He checked his phone for messages but there were none.

'GM451?' he shouted out. 'Where are you?' He got up and searched the hotel room but the spy dog was nowhere to be seen. 'Blast!' Switching on the tracker he located Lara's flashing red dot on-screen. 'Twelve miles due east,' he noted. 'It's time to call in a favour.'

He phoned the Secret Service and asked for Agent A. 'I wouldn't normally ask,' he said, 'but I need a helicopter . . .'

The blizzard was almost over as Lara looked down on the scene spread out below her. She watched three men walking to and from a shed and spied the lorry from the night before.

But where are the children?

Lara undid her backpack and emptied the contents on to the snow. She took the binoculars and scanned the magnified scene.

Wow! she whistled softly. She almost didn't see the rocket at first, its whiteness camouflaged against the snowy mountains. *That really is a huge rocket! But it looks as though the gas canisters are already attached. Maybe if I can find the kids then I might just be able to stop evil Jimmy's plans after all.*

Lara pointed the binoculars around the launch site.

'Gotcha!' she barked as she watched Sophie scamper into the log cabin and then back to a hiding place.

She looked at the men crowded around the rocket. *I've got to save the children. This spy dog needs a plan. And quick!*

18. Lift-off!

Lara scrambled down the hill towards the spot where Sophie had disappeared.

She gave a quiet woof. *Hi, guys,* she wagged, *fancy seeing you here!*

'Lara!' mouthed Sophie, beating her brothers to a hug. 'You're here. To rescue us. Everything's going to be all right.'

Not sure about that, she thought as she spied the men quickly heading back to the cabin.

'Five minutes and counting,' one of them shouted. 'Let's make ourselves scarce.'

'Five minutes!' yelped Ben. 'We've only got five minutes to stop the rocket!' The children stood looking up at the spacecraft. Its engines were rumbling into action, warming themselves before lift-off. A digital counter was counting down the seconds.

280, 279, 278 . . .

You guys, stay hidden, woofed Lara, using her paws to push them further into their hiding hole. *I've got to do something. Anything!*

'You can't stop the rocket,' said Ben. 'You'll get yourself killed.'

But I can release the gas canisters, barked Lara. *At least that way it's a harmless blast-off.*

Before they could stop her, Lara scurried down the snowy slope towards the rocket. The children watched as their pet stood upright and peered in through the cabin window.

The men are packing their bags, presumably for a quick getaway, Lara guessed. She spotted some tools hanging on the wall. *I need a spanner. Urgently.* The spy dog crept round the hut but the door was protected with a security code and the windows were locked shut. *Hmm, I'll have to try getting in from upstairs.*

Lara jumped on to the lorry cab and then on to its roof. She eyed up the next leap.

It's just about possible, she told herself, *if you believe a dog can fly!* Lara sprang for all her worth and scrabbled for a hold on the steeply sloping roof.

Sophie squealed from her hiding place as the children watched their pet start to slide down the roof in the snow. But Lara scrambled around and gradually hauled herself up towards the chimney.

It's the only way in! Lara stared down the hole into the blackness. *Well, if it's good enough for Santa, it's good enough for me.* The digital clock was ticking down. *Less than four minutes . . . No time to come up with another plan now.*

Ben gulped as he watched Lara disappear down the chimney. Ollie peered out from behind the gaps in his fingers.

'Ouch . . . ouch . . . eek . . . ouch . . . eek!' howled Lara before landing in the fireplace with an almighty *thud*. Soot filled the room and by the time the men realized what was happening a jet-black dog had opened the door and shot outside before it slammed behind her. Lara jumped up to the security keypad and pushed the Emergency Lock button.

'What's going on?' Jimmy shouted through the black cloud.

'A mutt's fallen down our chimney!' yelled one of the men. 'And it's stolen a spanner!'

Jimmy ran to the window and watched as Lara bounded towards *OZONE 1*.

'Do you want some even worse news, guys?' added one of the men, rattling the door handle. 'The bloomin' mutt's trapped us in here!'

All eyes watched as Lara raced to the rocket, a spanner in her jaws. The spy dog began to climb a metal ladder that ran the length of the rocket. She made it to the first gas canister and, hanging on with one paw, started to loosen the bolts.

'Go, Lara!' shouted Ben, coming out of the hiding place and jumping up and down with excitement.

'She's doing it!' squealed Sophie.

Ollie dared to open his eyes completely.

The men couldn't believe what they were seeing. 'Get yer shooter, Alex,' shouted one of them. 'That pesky mutt's stealing our gas.'

Lara twisted and twisted until the bolts came loose and canister number one fell to the ground. The rocket was shaking now in readiness for lift-off. The timer was ticking away . . .

122, 121, 120 . . .

Yikes, just two minutes to go!

Professor Cortex bowed his head and ran for the helicopter. The rotor blades were whipping up a snow storm and he slammed the cockpit door shut before indicating to the pilot to take off.

Two policemen were huddled inside, along with a medic.

'Up, up, man!' the professor bellowed to the pilot. 'To the mountains.'

★

The rocket engines on *OZONE 1* were now red hot. One of the men was clubbing at the locked door while another was pointing his gun out of the window.

'Careful you don't hit the rocket!' shouted Jimmy. 'Just get that crazy dog.'

The man aimed it at Lara and a shot rang out, the bullet pinging off the metal. 'I said be careful,' yelled Jimmy.

That was close, panicked Lara. *I have to work quicker. What other options do I have?*

The rocket was unsteady and her paw nearly missed the next rung. Ben, Sophie and Ollie gasped as their pet dangled from the rocket before grabbing on with her other paw and climbing to the second gas

canister. The twisting started again as more bolts flew off. Another bullet whistled past the rocket, just centimetres from her ear.

I've already got a hole in one, she thought, *so why not a matching pair!*

Lara checked the digital clock.

60, 59, 58 ... The second gas canister broke free and fell to the ground.

Phew. One to go!

The cabin door splintered open and the men rushed out, one waving a pistol. 'Hey, mutt, stop that,' he shouted. From the corner of her eye Lara saw him stride forward to get a better shot. 'I'm warning you,' he bellowed. 'Stop or I shoot again.'

'Can't stop, mister,' barked Lara out of the side of her mouth. *Less than sixty seconds to save the world.* She kept twisting the spanner around the final bolts.

The rocket was shaking violently, as if it were a rumbling volcano. The engines were breathing fire and the snow had melted around them. But the gunman continued forward, shading his eyes from the heat.

43, 42, 41 ...

The children looked on in horror from

above but were powerless to stop him as they watched him aim ... and pull the trigger. A shot rang out, as did the man's scream.

Ben, Sophie and Ollie watched in amazement as a dog in a superhero suit leapt at the man and sunk its teeth into his arm.

'Get off me, dog!' he bellowed, dropping his gun on the ground.

'Isn't that the arctic suit that Professor Cortex made?' Ben asked in amazement.

'Go, Lara,' barked Leo as he watched her climb to the final canister. 'I've got him.'

'Brilliant, Dad,' she barked back, dropping the spanner from her jaws.

Leo froze for a split second. *Dad?* he thought as he took a massive kick from the man. *Lara's my girl?* Suddenly Lara's interest in finding him made much more sense.

Sticky-up ear! Black and white. Clever like her mum ... it all makes sense.

The other man kicked at Leo, sending him sprawling to the ground. His friend recovered the gun and the Lycra-suited superdog leapt a second time. *Leave my daughter alone!* This time Leo couldn't stop the shot and he fell, turning the snow pink.

19, 18, 17 ...

Everyone watched as Lara struggled to loosen the final bolts with her teeth and claws. The heat from the engines was too much at ground level so the men had retreated, arms up against their faces. Lara struggled to hold on.

10, 9, 8 ... the first bolt fell away ...

7, 6, 5 ... she felt the second bolt loosen in her mouth ...

4, 3, 2 ... she spat the bolt out. *One to go!*

The children scrambled out of their hiding place as flames billowed from beneath the spacecraft and the earth shook. The digital clock registered zero and Lara hung on as *OZONE 1* lifted off.

'Ha ha,' the gunman shouted. 'We've won!

The rocket is launched and there's still one gas canister. That'll be enough to cause plenty of damage. And looks like that crazy dog is going into orbit too. Good riddance!'

But Lara wasn't giving up. As the rocket launched she hung on with one paw, working the final bolt with her teeth. *A couple more twists will do it.* She could see the children below. Ollie's hands had returned to cover his face. Sophie was screeching for Lara to jump. Ben was jumping up and down with panic.

The canister is rattling, almost loose. Oh my goodness! she wailed. *I might end up following my great-grandma into space!*

The children were getting smaller by the second. She twisted again and the final gas bottle fell to the ground with a crash. *Yessss!* She spat out the bolt, then let go of the rocket and fell with a huge doggie yowl. She watched the rocket disappear upwards and twisted to see the earth coming at her from below.

Very fast. Too fast! This is going to hur–

Lara landed in the deep Scottish snow with a *thud* and a yelp.

19. 'Make My Day!'

Lara lay still for a few seconds, watching the rocket disappear high into the sky. She made no attempt to move. She didn't even know if she could. Breathing seemed difficult enough. Eventually the rocket was just an orange speck of light before – *BANG!* – a huge explosion ripped it apart. Bright dots were spread across the grey sky. *Like fireworks!* Lara lay in her doggie-shaped snow hole, smiling at her success. She didn't mind the pain. *I couldn't stop the rocket*, she thought, *but I did stop Jimmy from destroying the ozone layer.*

Her thoughts turned to the children and her dad. Lara wiggled her paws to check they were working. She winced as she sat up in the snow hole, her head peering out over the scene. *Some singed fur and a sprained ankle. Oh, and a sore neck,* she thought, struggling to look left and then right. *Still, could have been much worse.*

A helicopter spluttered overhead and she saw the professor waving. Lara eased herself out of the snow hole and limped to her father.

Here, she said, pawing at Leo. *He needs medical treatment urgently, Prof.*

A rope ladder fell from the helicopter and figures started climbing down it.

'Dad,' barked Lara, above the noise. 'Dad, can you hear me?'

Leo opened his eyes and nodded. 'I hear you, girl,' he said. 'I knew you were special. That's why I came to do one last mission. But now I know just how special.'

'You're a hero, Dad.'

'Aye,' he agreed. 'I've even got the super-hero outfit to prove it.' Lara could see the pain in his eyes. Even a doggie smile was beyond him.

'You're so brave. Please hang on,' Lara whimpered. 'We've got some catching up to do. I love you, Dad.'

Leo spluttered and closed his eyes for a few seconds. 'Aye, Lara, and I've always loved you too,' he replied.

'Who's that dog in the professor's arctic suit, Lara?' asked Ollie.

'It's my father,' she barked, stroking his forehead and planting a lick on his cheek. 'And he's the bravest dog in the world.'

'Is everyone OK?' puffed Professor Cortex, struggling through the snow. Sophie and Ollie hugged the professor as the helicopter medic arrived with the police officers.

'We'll have to get him to the vet immediately,' he said.

'I can't save him but I may be able to capture *them*,' Lara barked, jabbing a paw at the three baddies who were escaping from the cabin.

'Over there!' shouted one of the policemen from the helicopter.

Lara was after the three men, her ears down, the slowest man in her sights. She took big three-legged bounds through the snow, her bad leg out of action. *This is exhausting.* She launched herself and grabbed his knees in the perfect rugby tackle. *Gotcha! Ben was right. You can't run without knees.* Lara sat on the man until one of the policemen caught up.

The children watched as the other two baddies made it to the lorry. Lara darted into the shed and came out holding a Taser gun. *How cool is this*, she thought, standing on her hind legs and holding the gun like she'd seen in the movies. Jimmy had retrieved a snowboard and was away down the mountain. Lara hated it when baddies escaped. She turned the Taser on his mate. *Go ahead, mister*, challenged Lara, *make my day!*

'You wouldn't,' stammered the man. 'I mean, you're a bloomin' dog!'

'Not any old dog,' growled Lara. 'I'm trained to catch baddies.' She pressed the gun's power button and it charged, ready to fire. The green light came on. *I'm not messing.*

You shot my dad. Either you put your hands up or I'll make your hair stand up. There're 5,000 volts waiting for you.

The man considered his options. The dog sure looked menacing. And it sounded angry. And it had powered up the gun. But it was only a dog ... and he knew dogs couldn't shoot guns.

Lara issued a warning growl. *Final warning, mister. Step away from the lorry.*

The man backed away, using his hands to calm the animal. 'Nice doggie,' he said. 'Put down the gun, doggie.'

Lara motioned the man over to the cabin. He walked backwards, hands held high. He was now standing underneath the steep snowy roof, right where Lara wanted him.

The man's patience finally snapped. 'OK, poochie,' he snarled. 'I'm calling your bluff. You're only a dog and dogs don't use stun guns.'

The man started to run for the lorry. Lara pointed the Taser at him and then raised the sights slightly before firing a bolt of electricity at the cabin roof. Lara was catapulted backwards into the snow. The blast of energy caused the snow on the roof to shift. An avalanche of snow fell with a *thud* and the man was stopped in his tracks.

Lara stood gingerly, her bad leg really hurting. Her head was spinning and she was seeing double. She noticed blood in the snow. *Must be the result of the fall from the rocket*, she thought. The man was buried up to his neck. She lowered the stun gun and beckoned to the police. *Dig him out*, she woofed. *Before the snowman catches a cold*.

The man's eyes were wild and his teeth were chattering. 'But you're only a dog,' he stammered.

A spy dog, growled Lara, her energy hitting zero.

Sophie squealed as Lara fell to her knees. By the time Ben had reached her, she had collapsed in the snow.

20. Serious Condition

Lara woke up and struggled to open her eyes. They stayed at half mast. She sniffed hard and grimaced. It didn't take a sensitive doggie nose to tell her she was probably in an animal hospital. She licked her dry lips and looked around. Her leg was suspended in the air, encased in white plaster. *Oops, that sore leg must have been more serious than I thought!* She could see her father lying in the next bed.

'Good morning, girl,' he smiled. 'Welcome back to the land of the living.'

'Dad,' she croaked. 'Are you OK?'

'Aye, Lara, I'll live,' he woofed. 'Which is more than we thought about you. Climbing a mountain in a blizzard, falling from a rocket and chasing baddies,' he explained.

'It's a miracle you only broke your leg. You hero! I'm so proud,' grinned her father.

'Just like you,' she smiled weakly. 'But what about the children?'

'The kids are fine,' began Leo, before the door was flung open and in raced Ollie, Sophie and Ben.

'Lara, you're awake,' yelled Ollie. 'We've been so worried about you, with your leg and everything.'

'And Leo's bullet wounds,' reminded Sophie. 'Check his ear, Lara, it's just like yours.'

Lara turned to her dad and smiled at the light shining through his sticky-up ear.

'Like father, like daughter,' he smiled.

The professor arrived and everyone went quiet. He frowned at Lara and lowered his eyebrows for one of his serious talks. 'Well, GM451,' he began. 'I hope you're proud of yourself. You've managed to get me in serious trouble with Mr and Mrs Cook. And I mean *serious* trouble, like never before. I told her it wasn't me, it was you and the rocket and saving the planet and all, but she wouldn't have it.'

Whoops, sorry, Prof, thought Lara, attempting a wag but finding it too painful.

'But, worst of all,' continued the professor, 'it's completely reckless of you to go mountaineering and rocket riding . . . in your condition!'

There was a moment's silence while everyone thought about the last sentence.

My condition?

'Her condition?' repeated Ben. 'What do you mean, "her condition"? She's retired, but you know adventures just come her way.'

'That's not what I mean, young Benjamin,' laughed the professor, unable to keep the grin from his face. 'Lara's going to have puppies. Quite soon, actually. She got the once-over from the doc and he reckons they're due in about six weeks. That explains why she's had such an appetite!'

Puppies? thought Lara excitedly. *I'm going to be a mum? Yippee!* she barked.

'And I'm going to be a grandad!' sang Leo. 'What wonderful news. I thought Lara finding me was exciting enough. I can't wait to tell them all my grandad stories about me being a superdog. And saving the planet, of course.'

Lara looked across at her dad with a big smile on her face and a warm feeling in her heart. *Hey, old dog,* she woofed, *WE saved the planet. And wait till I tell Potter he's going to be a dad!*

21. A New Beginning?

Mr Jetski was out of his room. The nurses considered it a miracle. He'd shuffled, unaided, to the TV lounge and was sitting watching the news.

'And check out this whacky adventure,' chuckled the newsreader to his partner. 'Two dogs climbed Scotland's highest mountain to stop a rocket that was being launched to wipe out the ozone layer. One of the dogs became a rocket rider, putting a stop to the evil plot masterminded by the man behind Jimmy's Tartan Suncream.' Footage from the helicopter was beamed to the nation. The camera was a bit wobbly but it clearly showed Lara riding the rocket before falling to safety. 'A very special doggie duo,' he added.

'Very special indeed,' chuckled Oleg Jetski,

clutching his framed picture. 'Laika would be so proud.'

Jimmy locked himself into the toilet cubicle and took the small mirror from his pocket. He peeled off his face and hair, removed his contact lenses and threw the whole lot into the toilet. He pressed the flush button and growled with anger as the wig floated in the toilet bowl.

'No matter.' Jimmy fixed the thick glasses to his face and opened the cubicle door. A young man had entered but an old one emerged. Jimmy bent double, playing the

role of the pensioner, and shuffled through to the airport departure terminal. He offered his passport to the official, who checked the picture before nodding him through.

'Enjoy your holiday,' smiled the passport control officer. 'See you again soon.'

'For sure,' croaked the old man. He had a plan that meant he'd be back for revenge. He had a spy dog to kill.

It was Lara's first neighbourhood watch meeting since the rocket episode. Her leg was still a bit wobbly but not as wobbly as her tummy.

'The pups are due any day,' reminded Potter. 'So take it easy, Lara!'

She limped out of the house, aided by the dad-to-be. Tears came to her eyes as the neighbourhood watch team stood and applauded.

'So good to have you back, boss,' yapped Rover, bouncing with enthusiasm. 'We saw you on the telly. What a hero! You're a rocket rider!' A dozen questions were barked and mewed at the same time.

'Quiet, quiet,' woofed Potter. 'Give Lara a

chance to speak. One question at a time please ... Beany,' he said, pointing to the whippet. 'You first.'

'What happened to the baddies?' asked the bug-eyed whippet.

'One was rugby-tackled at the mountain top,' winced Lara, remembering the pain in her leg. 'And I managed to capture the other in an avalanche.'

'And the mastermind behind the whole scheme? Jimmy the suntan-lotion man?' asked Jesse from number 4.

'His entire operation has been closed down,' Lara said happily. 'But unfortunately Jimmy managed to escape by snowboarding down the mountain. He's on the run, probably still up to no good. But do you know what? Scotland was just an experiment. If it was successful he was going to launch rockets to punch holes in the ozone layer over major cities throughout the world. The Secret Service found plans on his laptop for rockets over London, Sydney, Los Angeles and Paris. He would have made millions from his special suntan lotion.'

'Wow, what an evil man. I'm sure glad

he's out of our lives,' said Potter. 'But when our pups are born you'll have to stop having adventures, right? I mean it's too dangerous to keep getting into trouble.'

Lara smiled and gave Potter a friendly lick. 'I don't go looking for trouble,' she explained. 'It just sort of follows me around.'

'But puppies are important,' explained Potter. 'Surely the adventures will have to come to an end?'

Lara was lost in thought for a moment or two. 'Potter,' she woofed, 'I reckon puppies could be just the beginning!'

Spy Pups Family Fact File

Name: Laika
Nationality: Russian
The first dog in space, Laika was always thought to have died in orbit, but can it really be coincidence that GM451 has the very same silly ears and superbrain?

Name: Leo
Nationality: Scottish
Once strong as an ox, Leo is getting old these days, but it doesn't stop him from using determination to save Lara – and the day!

Name: Lara (Licensed Assault and Rescue Animal)
Nationality: British
The original Spy Dog! Skills include: karate, languages, typing with a pencil, driving cars, leadership – and more!

Name: Potter
Nationality: British
Lara's second in command, Potter is a good all-rounder: a sympathetic, intelligent dog with a positive attitude.

Bright and shiny and sizzling with fun stuff . . .

puffin.co.uk

WEB FUN

UNIQUE and exclusive digital content!
Podcasts, photos, Q&A, Day in the Life of, interviews
and much more, from Eoin Colfer, Cathy Cassidy,
Allan Ahlberg and Meg Rosoff to Lynley Dodd!

WEB NEWS

The **Puffin Blog** is packed with posts and photos from
Puffin HQ and special guest bloggers. You can also sign up
to our monthly newsletter **Puffin Beak Speak**

WEB CHAT

Discover something new EVERY month –
books, competitions and treats galore

WEBBED FEET

(Puffins have funny little feet and
brightly coloured beaks)

Point your mouse our way today!

It all started with a Scarecrow

Puffin is well over sixty years old.
Sounds ancient, doesn't it? But Puffin has never been
so lively. We're always on the lookout for the next big
idea, which is how it began all those years ago.

Penguin Books was a big idea from the mind of
a man called Allen Lane, who in 1935 invented
the quality paperback and changed the world.
**And from great Penguins, great Puffins grew,
changing the face of children's books forever.**

The first four Puffin Picture Books were hatched in 1940 and the
first Puffin story book featured a man with broomstick arms called
Worzel Gummidge. In 1967 Kaye Webb, Puffin Editor, started the
Puffin Club, promising to **'make children into readers'.**
She kept that promise and over 200,000 children became
devoted Puffineers through their quarterly instalments of
Puffin Post, which is now back for a new generation.

Many years from now, we hope you'll look back and
remember Puffin with a smile. **No matter what your age
or what you're into, there's a Puffin for everyone.**
The possibilities are endless, but one thing is for sure:
whether it's a picture book or a paperback, a sticker book
or a hardback, **if it's got that little Puffin
on it – it's bound to be good.**